Also

Holy Comfort

LEAVEN OF MALICE

*for Pat —
Enjoy these deeds of
dreadful note!
C.R. Compton*

C. R. Compton

HILLIARD HARRIS

P.O. Box 275
Boonsboro, Maryland 21713-0275

This novel is a work of fiction. Names, characters, places and incidents either are the product of the author's imagination or are used fictitiously. Any resemblance to actual persons, living or dead, events, or locales is entirely coincidental.

Leaven Of Malice Copyright © 2007 by C. R. Compton

All rights reserved. No part of this book may be reproduced or transmitted in any form or by any means, electronic or mechanical, including photocopying, recording, or by any information storage and retrieval system, without the written permission of the Publisher, except where permitted by law.

First Edition-June 2007
ISBN 1-59133-223-0
978-1-59133-223-7

Book Design: S. A. Reilly
Cover Illustration © S. A. Reilly
Manufactured/Printed in the United States of America
2007

For Sarah
"For there is no friend like a sister"

Acknowledgements:

Humble and hearty thanks for the encouragement to: Nicki Gillis, Sue and Bob Katsev, Harriet Reynolds, Jane Keough, Nancy Hawkins, Big Sleep Books, The good people of Grace Episcopal Church, Judie Schwartz, Karen Sterbenz, Leon McGahee, Sally Kopman, Louise Lonsbury and all my friends at the Lifelong Learning Institute, Mary Institute class of '74, Shawn and Stephanie Reilly, and most especially Mary, Wheeler, Susie and Paul Compton

Grant us to put away the leaven of malice and wickedness, that we may always serve thee in pureness of living and truth.
—Book of Common Prayer

Chapter 1

It was Friday. Roy Merton glanced across the seat at his partner Leona Vesba whose pale blue eyes were locked on the vanishing point toward which she guided her car. She chewed a wad of minty gum aggressively and with determination. He watched in sleepy awe the rhythmic movement of her jaw line. They had been called from their beds at an ungodly hour to hurry to a crime scene in Middle Essex, the oldest of the manicured suburbs that stretched westward from the river. Crime was not unknown there, but it was frowned upon as fundamentally déclassé.

"Big plans for the weekend, Roy?" asked Leona suddenly, startling her partner.

"No," he said, hoping to end the likelihood of a discussion with his tone. His eyes wandered to the window and to the flurry of dark leaves stirred up by Vesba's car. He turned back to his partner and checked his watch. It was almost 7:00 a.m. and still dark. He noted her pudgy fingers with their ridiculously long nylon nails. She could not even grasp the wheel efficiently without wounding herself. He smiled and out of the corner of his eye he caught a glimpse of the new moon in the eastern sky with Venus to the south, partnered on the brightening dark blue sky like symbols on an Arab flag.

"What are you staring at?" snapped Vesba.

"The moon and Venus," he said turning back to his own window.

"Flattery will get you nowhere, mister."

"No...I *meant* the moon and Venus..."

Vesba glanced over at her partner who looked to her like he was wearing the same clothes from the day before. Evidently he had not shaved again. "So what did you do last night?"

"I had a burger at the Trainwreck. I talked to the bartender."

"That doesn't explain your appearance." Merton looked down at his shirtfront. "You wore that yesterday," she said when he failed to respond.

"I wear this everyday," he said. "A blue shirt, this jacket, pants."

"You look like you slept in them."

"I didn't."

"Jesus. You used to take more pride in the way you looked."

"Leona, give me a break."

She noted the weariness in his voice but ignored it. "Why should I? Look at you. You're a goddam mess. Can't you get your hair cut at least? You look like a goddam hippie."

"I don't make personal comments about your appearance."

She threw a chilly look in his direction which he missed completely. "Damn straight," she said. Then she sighed meaningfully. "I don't know why I even bother to talk to you. You never listen to me. If you had, you'd never have hooked up with that ..."

"Leona," he said menacingly. "Please shut up."

"Don't use that tone with me and tell me to shut up."

"I believe I said 'please'."

"I've got a right to express myself in my own car," she said, refusing to let it go. "It's not natural to keep things bottled up inside yourself. You might feel better if you talked about your feelings once in a while. And contrary to popular opinion, I know you have them."

He threw his head back on the headrest. "You're right, I have feelings. Feelings of boredom, annoyance..."

"Oh, forget it." She braked abruptly and coasted. She gazed through the windshield. "Let's just try to focus."

"Where are we going anyway?"

"I told you. The Rochester-Bingham School. You might have dressed more appropriately."

He made a dismissive noise. "My Brooks Brothers suit is in mothballs."

"I guess so."

He leaned forward and opened the glove box. 'Do you still have that razor in here?"

"It's there. Keep looking."

He pulled the razor out from a thicket of personal items and switched it on. It made a reluctant buzzing noise. He reached up to the visor and pulled it down, then flipped the mirror open. He ran the razor lightly over his face and twice around his chin. "There," he said. "I guess that's better."

"Let me see," she said. He dutifully turned towards her.

"Jesus. You still look like something the cat dragged in." She made a clucking noise with her tongue as she turned her attention back to the road. Then she pointed straight ahead as the campus of the Rochester-Bingham School loomed ahead of them. She accelerated again and whipped the car around the corner, not bothering to stop at the intersection of Beasley Road and Middle Essex. She gunned the engine as she sped down Beasley looking for an entrance.

"Slow down, Leona," Merton suggested, bracing himself against the door and inwardly lamenting once again that she had bullied him into letting her drive. "Do you know where to turn? This place is huge."

"I was told to go to the 'South Campus'."

"Look," he said pointing to flashing lights in the middle of a long semi-circular driveway. "There."

Vesba grunted an acknowledgement, but slowed only slightly, taking the turn like a seasoned NASCAR driver. Ignoring the speed bumps, she accelerated to the flag-pole, then slammed on the brakes, executing a perfect 180-degree turn in front of what she assumed was the school entrance. "Shit," she hissed as she came to a stop. "I just got my wheels realigned."

Her partner did not comment.

Inside the building Merton crossed the black and white tiles of the chessboard front hallway, leaving his partner at the massive doorway talking to a uniformed policeman. He stopped at a large wooden, pedimented board covered with rows of small metal plaques engraved with names—hundreds of names—three names for each graduating class. He studied the names, which referred back practically to the nineteenth century and progressed until the early 1990s.

"What, may I ask, do you find so fascinating, Detective?" asked a voice at his shoulder. Merton looked down. A man of medium height, wearing horn-rimmed glasses, smirked beside him. In response he pointed to a name on a plaque almost at the bottom.

The other man leaned down. "Elizabeth Paget Browning—Academic Excellence. Is there a connection I'm missing?" he asked, smiling insincerely.

"Someone I know," said Merton. He stared at the man,

daring him to reply.

"Well, I'm afraid all that was before my time," he said, dismissing the entire wall of names with a wave of his hand. "Before the two schools merged. Ancient history."

Merton smiled down at the other man. He smiled because the man's use of unintentional irony amused him. "Yes," he said. "I suppose so. Are you the headmaster?"

"Forgive my manners. I'm George Crabtree," said the man with glasses. "Dean of students. You are?"

"Det. Roy Merton. Major Case Squad." He offered his hand and it was grasped limply and dropped again too quickly.

"Oh, of course." The man still looked puzzled, but he dismissed whatever was puzzling him and held out his hand toward a hallway. "The cafeteria is straight down those stairs. Then turn left. You can't possibly miss it."

Chapter 2

The cafeteria, thought Vesba, was not much to look at really—not for such a ritzy-ditzy place anyway. It was large and square with lots of long narrow windows lining up with rows and rows of long green tables and straight-backed green chairs. There were no curtains even. The walls were painted puke green. She certainly didn't have any desire to eat there, but no one gave a rat's ass what she thought about the décor of this particular lunchroom. She and her partner weren't there to eat. They were there to check out the body, and there it was—sprawled on the floor in the center aisle of the room. Vesba and her partner circled the body. The woman was old and fat—probably 180 pounds she guessed. Her hair, a dyed blonde bubble, was styled in such a way as to suggest that this lady had been wearing it that same way a long time, maybe 50 years even. Her dress, too, was not stylish. The word frumpy came immediately to mind. So this lady was evidently not into fashion. She was, however, wearing a mink coat (which bore the label of a high tone boutique that had been closed for twenty years) and a heavy gold necklace. She checked the dead woman's hands which clutched at her protruding abdomen. There were several large rings featuring impressive stones. Ah, she thought, she *was* into flaunting her wealth. Her purse lay unopened at her side. It looked like nothing had been stolen, so robbery did not appear to be the motive. Vesba squatted by the body to get a better look at the dead woman's face, frozen now in a ghastly grimace, her swollen tongue protruding, her eyes open. She reached for the purse and opened it with gloved fingers. Inside the satin lining she found a small coin purse and a monogrammed handkerchief, a cloisonné pillbox, a slim leather notepad and a tiny gold pencil. She flipped open the pad. On the first page were the words: *Crabtree, 10/7, 6:45 p.m., vulgar in my presence.* She closed the pad and returned it to the purse.

"Was this exactly how she was found?" Merton asked the uniformed policeman standing by.

"Exactly how," the man answered.

"Where's Jerry Altvater? Has he checked her out?" asked Merton.

"Sure has," said the policeman. "He's over there." He motioned with his head, indicating a dining table about halfway to the kitchen on the right side of the room where a bald man was hunched over writing in a patch of dim light.

"Thanks," said Vesba extending her hand so her partner would help her up. Her knees cracked as he did so and she groaned.

Merton and Vesba walked over and she lifted half of her buttocks onto the table by the Medical Examiner. Jerry Altvater looked over his glasses at her. "Good morning, Detectives," he said.

"So what happened to the old broad, Jer?" said Vesba. "Did she see a ghost?"

The M.E. smiled ever so slightly. "No ghosts, Leona."

"Then what?" she asked pulling the other half of her buttocks onto the table and crossing her legs.

The M.E. cleared his throat and leaned back. He threw down his pen. "Judging from the position of her body on the floor, I'd say she suffered from convulsions. Ultimately she choked to death on her swollen tongue. She may have gone into a coma for a short time. I'd estimate she died between 8:30 and 9:30 p.m."

"What caused the convulsions and the...tongue?" asked Merton.

"Any number of things. A seizure. Perhaps she was an epileptic."

"Natural causes, then?"

Altvater shook his head slowly. "It might have been she was poisoned."

"Why? Did you find anything?"

"No. CSU searched the area around the body. So far, nothing. I'll be able to tell you what she ingested after I do an autopsy. I'll call you as soon as I know anything." He closed his notebook and stood up.

"Jerry," said Merton as he turned with the M.E. to look across the room at the disheveled body on the floor. "If someone poisoned her, did they poison her here or somewhere else? How long..."

"Some poisons are very fast-acting. We'll know for sure after I study the contents of her stomach."

"No guesses?"

"I don't like to guess, Roy."

"We won't tell, Jer," said Vesba as she hopped off the table, using her hand on Jerry's blue wool shoulder for balance.

The M.E. smiled. "There is a purple stain on the woman's upper lip, as if she took a bite of a fruit tart. Some fruit seeds are highly poisonous and act similarly to cyanide. It might be she was poisoned right in here in the cafeteria and experienced a violent reaction to whatever she ate. It may have taken her awhile to die, however."

Vesba nodded. "Could it have been an accident?"

"You mean could she have wandered down here and found a poisoned fruit tart, eaten it and died?"

"Well, gee, when you put it like that..."

Altvater smiled again and looked down. "No, if she was poisoned, it was no accident, but someone cleaned up the area pretty well. There's no sign of the fruit tart except the stain over her lip. They were hoping probably we'd assume a seizure of some sort. Murderers always hope for the best."

"And we always expect the worst," said Vesba.

"It must have been someone she knew," said Merton, who wasn't listening.

"Someone she knew and trusted," said Vesba, refocusing.

"Yes," agreed the M.E. "After cleaning up, he or she left the victim to die."

"Nice," said Merton.

"You'll let us know as soon as you figure out what killed her?" asked Vesba, poking the M.E.'s shoulder with a long-nailed finger.

"Sure. No problem," said Altvater, running a hand over the smooth top of his skull.

"Who found the body?" Merton asked.

"The woman over there I believe," said Altvater pointing. He indicated a small woman sitting at one of the long green tables. Vesba thanked him and, motioning to her partner, headed over to the woman, who looked up as they approached.

"My name is Tina Rosales. I work in the kitchen," she said before they had a chance to ask. Both detectives nodded, and Merton smiled.

"Did you come in early this morning, Ms. Rosales?" asked Vesba.

"It's Friday. I always come in early on Fridays to start the yellow rolls. These kids, they got to have their yellow rolls on Friday."

"Sure. I guess they do," said Vesba nodding. She glanced at her partner skeptically.

"So I come in around 5:30...I come through the back, into the kitchen direct...I never notice her, the dead woman, until later, almost 6 o'clock. Then I scream and knock over a tray of glasses." She crossed herself, and then pointed to a neat pile of broken glass.

"It must have been a shock," said Merton.

"Sure it was a shock. I never see no dead body before. I see a kid fall out a window once—over there from the third floor into the courtyard—backwards like she just lean back and...but she don't die. She not even crippled. She probably so high she bounce."

"Drugs?" interrupted Vesba. "The kids use a lot of drugs here?"

"Sure. I see a kid selling another kid drugs. These kids, they're no angels, believe me, and they got the money to buy what they want. They go around high all the time."

"Did you see anyone this morning?" asked Merton. "Anyone at all?"

"No. The place is deserted—still dark. I wave to Mike the security guard when I pull in the parking lot. There are no other cars."

"What about her car?" asked Vesba pointing to the deceased.

Tina Rosales shrugged. "I don't see cars."

Chapter 3

"Red sky at morning," said the tall man looking out the nine-foot windows at the red sky. "Sailors take warning."

Merton did not agree or disagree. He did not comment at all. He stood calmly and waited with his partner to be asked to sit down. They waited for several minutes before Vesba cleared her throat, emphatically and wordlessly reminding the headmaster of the Rochester-Bingham School of their presence. Then Thurgood "Buzz" Pinchot turned around. He was tall and what passed for good-looking. He looked as if he had taken a shower and combed his blonde hair back, the ridges from the comb still visible. Something about the set of his broad shoulders suggested annoyance. He paused, then extended his hand to Vesba who took it and shook it once. "Detectives?" he asked.

"Yes," said Merton, grasping Pinchot's hand. He introduced himself and his partner and tried to hold the other man's eyes with his own gaze. The headmaster refused to allow a connection, only glancing at them in a dismissive manner that both detectives noted. Then he smiled half-heartedly and gestured to the three chairs in front of his desk. "Sit down," he said. "Please. Sit down."

They all sat down in black captain's chairs which featured the school's crest emblazoned in gold on their backs. "What's happening here, Detectives? What's this about Ethel Weinrich...being found dead...in the cafeteria...They say..."

"Who says?" asked Merton, calmly crossing his long legs.

"George...George Crabtree, my dean, says. He got here before I did. He told me."

"I see," said the detective.

"But I don't quite see, Detectives. Is she dead? Is Ethel dead?"

"Yes," said Merton. "She's dead. She died in the school cafeteria some ten hours ago."

"In the cafeteria? For god's sake, what was she doing there?"

"We were hoping you could tell us, Sir."

The headmaster grumbled. "Why would Ethel Weinrich choose the school cafeteria to die in? She always hated it. She hated the color green, the ivy trim, the *smell* of the food..."

"We didn't say that she chose it, sir," said Merton interrupting.

"What?"

"She didn't choose to die in the cafeteria," said Vesba. "Someone else chose it. She was murdered."

"*Murdered?*" whispered Pinchot.

"It looks that way," said Vesba. "We won't know for certain until an autopsy has been performed."

"I see," muttered the headmaster.

"We'd appreciate your filling us in a little," said Merton. "If you could tell us what you know about the deceased, about Ethel Weinrich."

Thurgood Pinchot raised his round blue eyes and stared at Merton as if he had been speaking in some strange Eskimo dialect. "What?" he asked.

"Mrs. Weinrich. The dead lady," interrupted Vesba. "What do you know about her?"

"Ethel?" he asked again. Both detectives nodded indulgently. The headmaster cleared his throat. "She was a graduate of Rochester Hall, class of 1950 or 1951. She was a loyal alumna and a great patron of the school. Over the years she and her husband, Carl, had been very generous..."

"How generous?" asked Vesba. "Thousands? Hundreds of thousands?"

"Millions," said Pinchot, his blue eyes staring. "Millions of dollars. They built the black box theater and the dance studio at Rochester Hall, now the south campus. However, when the two schools merged—Rochester Hall and Bingham Country Day—Ethel was very unhappy. She withdrew her support. She didn't like the headmaster, Fred Twain, at all. She didn't like anything he did."

"Then when you came on board..." Vesba prompted.

"Yes, four years ago. She warmed up a little. Carl had passed away by then...She liked me. She was going to..."

"She was going to what?" asked Vesba when he paused.

"She was going to kick off the capital campaign with a very generous gift..."

"How much?" asked Vesba as she crossed her fat legs, splicing the air with the distinctive sound of nylon against nylon.

Pinchot looked at her, an expression of dread, not sorrow, creasing his broad face. "Five million," he said. "She was going to give me five million."

"Give *you* five million?" asked Vesba leaning forward, seeking his eyes.

The headmaster looked away and waved his hand vaguely in the air. "Just a figure of speech...Of course, she was going to give the *school* five million. I made the ask, so I thought of it as my gift."

"And now..." said Merton.

Pinchot raised his eyes sharply. "And now? And now who knows. It was a verbal agreement, you understand. We had only talked...Nothing was in writing yet..."

"I see," said Merton. "Was there any problem with her gift—any strings attached that might have caused problems?"

"Problems?" Pinchot asked dully. "Strings? There are always strings—Ethel wanted...She didn't like the architectural design as planned with the new administration building as a bridge between the north and south campuses. She never liked the idea of the two schools merging. She wanted them separated—geographically at least. So she came up with the idea that a small area between the schools—some trees and a pond—should be preserved as a park, named, of course, after her late husband. She was adamant about it. The administration building could just be built somewhere else. She didn't care where. It didn't matter to her that we'd already spent a quarter of a million dollars in preliminary architectural planning. What was that to her? Some of her friends had already contacted the National Arbor Society about the trees. They said they were endangered. Can you believe it? It was rubbish, of course." The headmaster paused and passed his hand across his mouth. He had begun to perspire. He stood up and moved to the window. "She didn't care about any of that anyway. It was just a power move to demonstrate who was in control. She didn't really care about trees, for god's sake. She didn't care about anything."

"Anything?" asked Merton.

The headmaster crossed his arms and looked out the window.

"Well, she cared about her position, her reputation. She cared about being respected. Ever since Carl died, she'd been...throwing up walls wherever she could...trying to slow down time, to stop things from changing."

The detectives waited, but Pinchot was silent, seemingly deep in thought.

"Well, what can you tell us, sir, about last night?" asked Vesba finally.

Pinchot looked startled. "What?"

"Why was Mrs. Weinrich here last night?" asked Merton.

"We had a board meeting last night. Ethel was here, but she left...about 8:30. She didn't return."

"Where did she go?" asked Vesba.

"How should I know?" snapped Pinchot. He crossed his arms in front of his chest again and sucked in his cheeks. "She was a grown woman—she could leave if she chose to. I wasn't going to chase after her."

"Even for 5 million dollars?" challenged Merton.

"No!" said Pinchot, disgusted, as his hands flew to his sides and he half-turned to the detectives. "Ethel Weinrich was like that. She'd stomp out like a petulant child. I'd learned to let her go..."

"Did anyone else follow her?"

The headmaster passed his hand over his mouth again. "Come to think of it, Renzi Stark followed her out. And shortly after that, George Crabtree suggested we all take a break. I saw Stark talking on his cell phone in the hall. After the break everyone came back except Ethel...We broke up around 10 o'clock."

Merton finished writing in his notebook and closed it. He looked up at the man who had returned to stand behind his desk. "Thank you for your cooperation, sir," he said rising to his feet. "We'll need a list of everyone who attended the meeting."

"Yes, of course," muttered the headmaster.

"Are you canceling school today?" asked Vesba.

"What?" said the other man. "I'm sorry. What did you say?"

"I asked you if school has been canceled."

"Oh, yes, quite so. George was taking care of that... Automated phone calls to all households. Had to cancel, of course...we couldn't have the children..."

"You'll have the weekend to get things back in order," suggested Vesba who had risen from her chair. She picked up a framed picture on the desk and studied it. A blond woman and four apple-cheeked children in matching sweaters smiled blandly at the camera. "Your family?" she asked.

"What?" the headmaster asked again. "I'm sorry?"

"Your family," she repeated handing him the photo to jog his memory.

He stepped over to the desk and took the picture from Vesba. "Yes," he said curtly. "That's Mary Farrell and our children." He put the picture down on the desk and, looking up, smiled at the detective. "If there's anything I can do for you to help in any way, please, just give me a ring." He stretched out his hand to shake.

Chapter 4

"So you've seen the body?" asked Merton.

"Yes," said George Crabtree. "It was a terrible shock I can assure you. Absolutely shocking." He adjusted his glasses and folded his hands on his lap. He looked anything but shocked.

"Shocking yes. But how is it that you got here before Mr. Pinchot? Doesn't he live on campus?" asked the detective.

"Yes. He does—up the hill behind the athletic fields on the south campus. But it's a big campus—it would take a little while. And Buzz never moves fast anyway. He takes his time."

"But still—do *you* live on campus?" the detective asked.

"No. Buzz paged me. I wasn't home."

"Where were you then, if not at home?"

"Does it really matter? It's rather private."

"It matters," said Vesba, cutting in impatiently. "Where were you?"

"I was...at a friend's house."

"Which friend?" asked Merton.

The dean sighed and raised his eyes to gaze at the ceiling. "Mason Holt's—She's a good friend, and she's depressed. I was just..."

"Holding her hand?" interrupted Vesba. "And where does *she* live?"

"Across the street actually...on Glen Quarry Road."

"Had you been holding her hand all night?" asked Vesba.

The dean scowled. "I'd been there since the board meeting broke up around 10 o' clock. I gave her a lift home."

"Are you married, Mr. Crabtree?" asked Merton.

"I'm separated," said the dean. Vesba exhaled noisily and he colored slightly. "What does any of this have to do with Mrs.

Weinrich's murder?"

"An alibi—You want one, don't you?" said Vesba. "We'll have to check with Ms. Holt."

"Fine. I'm telling the truth, of course."

"Of course," said Merton agreeably. "Do you always go to board meetings?"

"Yes. Buzz likes to have back-up, moral support."

Merton nodded. "How does someone get elected to a seat on the board?"

"There's a nominating committee. People are chosen based on the amount of money they've given to the school, their social position in the community. We try to keep a balance between parents, former parents, alums, etc. There are two appointed positions—the co-presidents of the Alumnii Association. Those two automatically go on for a two-year term when they become co-presidents."

Vesba checked her list. "And who are they?"

"Cassie Cavanaugh, who represents Rochester Hall, and Renzi Stark, the Bingham Country Day School. One of these days we'll get beyond this childish tradition of having to have 'one girl'/'one boy' for every position—but it'll take awhile. Especially if Renzi Stark has his way." The dean's tone was impatient and he fairly spat the name.

"Why especially Renzi Stark, may I ask?" said Vesba squinting slightly.

"Because Renzi Stark's forever looking back, back, back to the golden years. Good god, he only went to the school for a few years. It's really rather pathetic."

"Is he an old guy?" asked Vesba sympathetically.

"Renzi? He isn't a day over 35. No—It's just that old Renzi never surpassed those high school glory days playing football, throwing touchdown passes. Ra Ra. It nearly killed him when we changed the school colors and retired that mangy bulldog." The dean laughed and neatened the stack of paper in front of him on the desk.

"A moral victory for you," said Merton.

"Well, yes," the dean said continuing to snicker. Then he stiffened. "How else can I help you, Detectives? I do have a lot of work to do."

"Of course you do," said Merton staring across the desk. He paused. "Did everyone on the board get along with Mrs. Weinrich? Did she have any enemies?"

"Getting along with Ethel Weinrich wasn't the easiest thing to do," said the dean. "You have to understand, she could be...argumentative. She liked to be in control. When you have 150 million dollars that usually isn't a problem, but...people were sick of it—the way she always had to have the final say. And she would change her mind. She had promised Buzz five million. It was a done deal—verbally, of course—then she comes up with that park idea. 'A brotherhood of venerable trees' she called it. She was contacting the National Arbor Society!"

"People took her seriously?" said Vesba.

"You bet they did. There was fire-power behind her threats. She single-handedly kept Wal-Mart out of Middle Essex!"

"When Ethel Weinrich left the meeting last night, why did you suggest a break?" asked Merton.

"The air was fraught with tension," said the dean looking owlishly from behind his glasses. "And besides, I had to go to the john." He smiled again.

"What was causing the tension?"

"Ethel, of course. She was on her soapbox once again about the *trees,* God's blessed trees. The thing is, everyone knew she didn't give a hoot about any trees. She wanted Buzz to beg her for the five million. She wanted him on his knees."

"But why?" asked Vesba.

"Why?" asked the dean narrowing his eyes. "Because she could make him. What other amusements did she have?" The dean contemplated his tented fingers. "I hear she was threatening Renzi Stark as well...If he didn't side with her, he'd lose his job...You see, he works for the family law firm. It's all very incestuous. That's how the game is played."

"Who told you about Renzi Stark?" asked Merton.

"Mason Holt as a matter of fact."

"Well, on that note," said Vesba as she stood up and adjusted her tight skirt. "If you'll excuse me, I've got to powder my nose." She turned, waving her hand to signal her contempt on her way out the door.

"A charming lady," said the dean. "Isn't it wonderful to see women making their mark in the workplace?"

"Thank you for your time," said Merton. He stood up and turned to leave, but was stopped by Crabtree's hand on his shoulder. How he had slipped around his oversized desk so quickly was a mystery, but there he was standing at the detective's side, looking up, barely suppressing a smile.

"Oh, Detective," said the dean. "I looked up your friend—Elizabeth Paget Browning. She's the one whose ex-husband committed those ghastly murders over at Holy Comforter. I suppose you became *friends* during the investigation..." The man's insincerity was palpable.

Merton nodded. "Goodbye," he said, then turned and covered the space to the door in two long steps.

"Glad to help," sneered the dean. But the detective was already gone.

Chapter 5

Vesba slammed the door and wrenched the seatbelt across her abdomen, jamming the lock in place. Her partner eased into the passenger seat and buckled his seatbelt. As if she could feel his smile, she lowered her shoulders and exhaled loudly. "God, I get sick of his type, don't you?"

Merton shrugged. "They're hard to avoid."

"I'd like to know who he thinks made him cock of the run? Little runty asshole."

"Leona."

"All right. I'll calm down," she said, but her knuckles were white as she gripped the steering wheel. "Guys like him, looking down their long pointy noses, thinking they're so much smarter that we are, just make my skin crawl."

"I take it you didn't feel that way about Buzz Pinchot?" asked her partner.

She released the steering wheel and glanced sideways at Merton. "Okay, I kind of liked him. He had feelings anyway. What about you?"

"I'm not sure," said Roy. "Something about him didn't seem right. He was trying too hard...acting the part of the shell-shocked administrator."

"I didn't sense that."

"No? You didn't think he was laying it on a little thick? He'd obviously talked to Crabtree, but he wanted us to believe he didn't know anything." Vesba said nothing as she drummed her fingers on the steering wheel. "He seemed overly distracted..."

"The news must have been a terrible shock," she said. Merton grumbled in response. "Uh huh," Vesba grumbled back.

He turned to face her. "And another thing. Did he touch your ass as we were leaving?"

Vesba's hand flew around and punched him in the arm. "No, he did not!" She crossed her arms and stared out the window.

Merton rubbed his arm and smiled, gazing at the school. The sun had risen and in the light of day the school was clearly visible where before the detective had only noted the existence of a stone staircase leading to a covered portico and massive glass doors. Now the full impact of the impressive brick building with its six sturdy pillars struck him suddenly. "This place is huge," he said, startled into declaration.

"No shit," said Vesba as she shifted in her seat.

"I've never really taken a good look at the place—driving by I mean. It's like a small college or something." He whistled to emphasize his point.

"Yeah big deal," she said. "Don't start on some big thing about the stupid school. I could care less. It's just a rabbit hutch for rich kids as far as I'm concerned."

"Okay," he said. "What put you in such a bad mood this morning? Were you up too late with Jerry or what?"

She turned slowly. "What are you talking about? Jerry who?"

He raised an eyebrow. "Jerry Altvater from the Medical Examiner's office."

She hit the steering wheel. "How'd you know? It's because I've gained a little weight isn't it? I always gain weight when I'm happy."

"It's all over the department," he said. She groaned. "Who'd you tell?"

She shrugged. "I may have mentioned it to Helene Geisel."

"Not a smart move." He paused. "Why didn't you tell me?"

"I thought maybe...well, everyone knows your love life sucks."

"And you thought I'd be jealous? Thanks for being so thoughtful."

"I was trying to be sensitive," she said. "Everything started coming together with us not long after the shit hit the fan with you and..."

"I hear you," he said. "Is this serious?"

"I've got an open mind."

Merton nodded. "Jerry's on the rebound, you know."

"I know," she said impatiently. She sat up straight and put her hand on the gear shift.

"He's not divorced yet…"

"Don't worry—my expectations are reasonable, unlike some people's."

Roy did not flinch, but just looked out the window. She sighed. "I guess we should talk to this Renzi Stark character."

"Eventually, but let's go see Mason Holt first since she's just across the street. Then we'll swing by Mrs. Weinrich's house and see what the crew there has turned up. Her son is supposed to meet us over there."

"I can hardly wait—another asshole lawyer."

"Forbear to judge," said Merton, leaning back in his seat and closing his eyes. "For we are sinners all…And let us all to meditation."

"Yeah, right, meditate on this," replied Vesba. "What the hell are yellow rolls?"

LEAVEN OF MALICE

Chapter 6

George Crabtree smiled at the headmaster's bewildered secretary, then tapped once on the door to his office and opened it. Buzz Pinchot turned from the window where he stood staring and nodded to his associate. He did not smile or acknowledge his presence further. Crabtree sat down and thought to himself what a really nice office Pinchot had and how much he would enjoy sitting on the other side of his desk. He sighed and cleared his throat.
Finally Pinchot sat down. "Did you speak with the detectives, George?" he asked.
"Sure I did. They're not exactly what I've come to expect from television."
Pinchot ignored the dean's remark. "I suppose I should call David Whittier and let him know what's happened. See whether the school is liable for any damages…"
George Crabtree nodded and studied the other man's profile. Pinchot seemed tired, as if he had been swimming against a strong current for a long time. "Buzz," he said. "Can I get you anything? It's a bit early for a drink, but under the circumstances…"
"I think not," snapped the headmaster. "I'm fine. It's just…"
"The shock, I know," said Crabtree finishing his sentence.
"No, George," said Pinchot, a thin edge of annoyance creeping into his voice. "I was going to say that I keep picturing Ethel Weinrich—poor Ethel—snatching her fur coat as she left the Blankenship Room for the last time saying, 'It's as cold as the morgue in here. Can't we afford to turn the heat on anymore?' That was the last thing she ever said to me."
"How appropriate that she was complaining," muttered Crabtree.
"It's ironic, don't you think, that she mentioned the morgue?

Little did she know that she'd be *in* the morgue less than 24 hours later." The headmaster looked over Crabtree's head at a point in the distance, barely aware of his presence.

The dean looked at his boss, scrutinizing his ruddy, open face. "It's odd you know, I went to the john and then to my office where I met Mason, and we walked back to the Blankenship Room. We never saw anyone lurking in the shadows, just Renzi Stark talking on his cell phone."

"*Renzi Stark*," said Pinchot, annoyed again. "Renzi Stark. Wouldn't it be just too convenient if *he* was the one who'd murdered Ethel?"

"Are they so sure it was murder, Buzz?" interrupted Crabtree.

"Well, I...the way the detectives talked...all the questions they asked," stammered Pinchot. The two men stared at each other. "They as much as said she was murdered."

Crabtree smoothed his gray flannel leg. "They asked me if Ethel had many enemies, but they seemed more concerned with my social life than anything else." He chuckled and mumbled something about idiots.

Pinchot blinked. "Renzi Stark indicted for murder. It would be well worth the public relations hell to kill those two birds with one stone..."

"Jesus, Buzz," said Crabtree as he surveyed the ceiling. "No, my idea of two birds with one stone would be if somehow that secretary of Ethel's had been pinned as well. Good lord, remember her? When she used to come to the board meetings with Ethel? She was always trying to insinuate herself, make her presence known somehow. I suppose Ethel felt special having her private secretary along, but good god, they were hard to stomach."

The headmaster smiled blandly and folded his hands on the desk. "Well, I suppose those detectives will sort this all out..."

"Maybe. I can't say they inspired a great deal of confidence in me."

"No? Appearances, George, can be deceiving."

Crabtree shifted in his seat. "That is very true, Buzz. In point of fact, one of those detectives actually knows a Rochester Hall alum."

"Really?" drawled Pinchot, momentarily distracted from his low spirits. He smiled, revealing his dimples. "The cowboy?"

"Yes. He says he's acquainted with Page Browning, Rochester class of eighty-something. Her name is on the board in the front hall. Do you know her?"

"Browning? I know Sally Browning Phillips. I'm going to her birthday party on Saturday night as a matter of fact. I can't say I even knew she had a sister."

"I looked her up. She gave to the school jointly with her husband—nice gifts too—but stopped, I assume, when they divorced. Nothing since." He waited, but the headmaster appeared to have nothing to say. "It does make you wonder, Buzz...the smartest girl in the class, from a family with all the connections...making a police detective go all misty-eyed. Her ex-husband was the one who killed those people over at Holy Comforter. You remember what a mess that was. But we did get a nice gift from the estate of Bradford Cole..."

The headmaster did not seem to be listening. He gazed at his hands and said, "I like *Sally*. She's a pretty little thing with a very rich husband."

Then he looked directly at his dean and laughed. He tipped his head back and opened his mouth wide. The dean joined him, laughing heartily.

Chapter 7

Mason Holt opened the door and welcomed the detectives into her home with the practiced warmth of a game show hostess. No warnings about skin cancer and ultraviolet rays and connections with the aging process had ever scared her, thought Vesba. It appeared as well that Ms. Holt agreed with the pop adage that you couldn't be too rich or too thin. The woman was positively skeletal. The detective sighed and sucked in her own stomach as she tugged at her tight skirt.

"Thank you for agreeing to see us, ma'am," said her partner. He had a smooth way with women like this. Boy, did he ever. Vesba watched him as she allowed herself to be led to an immense room at the back of the house with a two-story cathedral ceiling and skyscraper windows. Through those windows she could see a pool and a tennis court and what appeared to be a putting green. She settled back in the beige chair she had been directed to take. It was comfortable, but she had her doubts about ever getting out of it again. She looked around. This was a huge house, as big as a dorm, but as far as she could tell, home only to the woman before her, who was noting the time on her wristwatch.

Merton leaned forward in his chair and stared at Mason Holt. "George Crabtree tells us he spent the night here last night. Is that true?"

"How extremely ungallant," she said, stressing the last syllable.

"Maybe," said Merton, also stressing the last syllable. "Is it true?"

"Yes, it's true. The dear man brought me home after the board meeting. I had such a headache! We talked and talked. How terrible to think that while we were talking, *that* was going on at the school. And we had no idea!"

Merton nodded. "How well did you know Mrs. Weinrich?"

"Ethel and I sat on several boards together over the years and we went to the same church. However, we belonged to different generations." She pulled a needlepoint pillow on to her lap and hugged it. "Change came hard for Ethel. The schools merging was sort of the last straw for her. I think she saw this park idea of hers as her final act of defiance. The world be damned, you know. But she was old and tired of fighting, and there was no one to pass the baton to. No one agreed with her anymore—no one who mattered. She hadn't grown with the times. I mean there are some very lovely Asian and Pakistani doctors' families at the school now, and we try very hard to find qualified African-American children to apply. But Ethel could never see the need to diversify our student body. She thought the idea of inclusiveness was absurd at a private school. We are exclusive by our very nature she would say. Can you imagine?"

"Yes," he said. "I mean no." He coughed. "Did anything unusual happen at the meeting?"

"Unusual?" she repeated. "No, just the usual endlessly tedious discussions about the same old things."

"No arguments?"

"Of *course*, but those are becoming old hat too. I mean, what would a meeting *be* without Renzi Stark dredging up the good old days and school TRADITIONS and how we should keep the past always in our minds as we inch ever so carefully forward. Sometimes, if it would support her own stance, Ethel Weinrich would agree with him. It's ironic really."

"Why ironic?" snapped Vesba, unable to keep quiet any longer.

"Well," said the other woman, momentarily aware of Vesba. "This time, when it was really important to Ethel, Renzi disagreed. He was supportive of the plans to build the new administration building. He went along with the idea of bridging the two schools. In fact, he had words with Ethel on that very subject. I believe she told him his opinion wasn't relevant, that in fact *he* wasn't relevant. She sort of went off on him. Nobody disagreed either."

"Did she say that last night?" asked Merton.

"No. She said it at the meeting last month...in September. Nobody likes to be told they're not relevant, even if it's true. *Especially* if it's true, I guess." She stopped. "Renzi was pretty quiet last night, come to think of it."

"And *that* was unusual?" asked Merton making a note in his

spiral book.

"Renzi not talking was unusual. He was so proud of himself—being on the big board, you know. Big Deal. It wasn't, of course. Nobody cared about Renzi Stark or what he thought."

"Why not?"

"Well," she said, rattling the jumble of gold bracelets on her wrist. "Talk, talk, talk—that's all there is to Renzi Stark. His father was a car dealer, you know—and not a very successful one either. Buicks, I think, or *Pontiacs*. Anyway, Renzi just has professional money of his own—There's no depth there."

"No depth?"

"No. I tell you, there won't be any significant gifts in the future from him."

"And that's what a seat on the board is all about?" asked Vesba.

"Well, it can work the other way, you know. Renzi might have made it work for himself, if he'd just played the game. But he made a big mistake during his short tenure in the Big Time. He made an enemy of Ethel Weinrich." She leaned forward slightly to emphasize her next point. "I heard she threatened him—his job, you know. He works for the Weinrich firm. All she had to do was tell Carl Jr. to fire him and his career would be toast."

Merton looked at his partner, his eyebrows raised. She shrugged in answer to his non-verbal question. He stood up and the two women joined him. "I guess that's all, Ms. Holt. For now."

Mason shrugged. "Well, do call, Detectives, if you think of anything else." She reached for his hand. "You know, I've just now realized who you are. You solved those murders over at Holy Comforter last year. You're the friend of the sister of an old friend of mine—Sally Browning. You're friends with Page Browning *Hawthorne*." She said the words accusingly, as if she had caught him in the act of stealing something.

He said nothing, his face a mask again.

She squared her shoulders contritely, but did not let go of his hand. "That was certainly terrible—all that terrible...I mean who would have thought that Chester Hawthorne was capable of murder? And then what he did to poor Page! We all felt just terrible for Page." Her eyes never left the detective's face, probing for a weak spot, as she made a clucking noise with her tongue. "A good plastic surgeon should be able to fix her right up though. They can do great things with scars these days."

Merton took back his hand and turned to his partner. "We'd better be going."

"Well, if that's all I can do for you," said Mason Holt sweetly.

Chapter 8

Surprisingly, Carl Weinrich, Jr. himself opened the door to his mother's large brick residence and invited the detectives to enter. They introduced themselves and apologized for intruding. "We're sorry for your loss, sir," said Merton as Vesba nodded her agreement.

"Thank you, Detectives," said Carl Weinrich, a tall bald man who spoke without emphasis and moved slowly. "I've just gotten back from the school. They called me to come to…to see Mother. It was ghastly. I'm afraid I'm a bit shaken up." He turned away from the sympathetic eyes of the detectives and led them into a small room off the living room in which there was a large dark desk and a wall of bookshelves and file cabinets behind louvered doors. In the corner stood a thin middle-aged woman in a plain navy suit. She clutched her hands nervously and scowled.

"This is Sylvia Arno, my mother's secretary," said Carl Jr. "Sylvia, these are the detectives from the Major Case Squad. Was it Merton and Vesba?"

Sylvia relaxed her hands and offered her right one to each detective in turn. "How do you do?" she asked, nervously touching the brown bun at the base of her skull.

"We're sorry for your loss, ma'am," repeated Merton.

Sylvia nodded and turned to Carl Jr. who cleared his throat. "We were just about to open the safe when you arrived," he explained as he stepped to the west wall and removed a small oil painting of a large cocker spaniel. He began fingering the combination dial and momentarily pulled the door open. "Oh," he groaned as Sylvia Arno's shoulders tensed. "I was afraid of this."

Carl Jr. turned around. He held a plain white envelope in his hands. He extracted a smaller yellow envelope from inside.

"May I?" said Merton, extending his hand. Carl Jr. hesitated, but handed the envelopes over.

Merton pulled out a handful of photographs and looked at the first three or four, then handed them to his partner. "Do you know who the people in the pictures are?" he asked.

Carl Jr. looked at the beige-carpeted floor and dug his toe into an old stain. "The girl is my daughter, my 15-year old daughter Julie. The man is her English teacher, Stuart Bunting."

"You've seen these before?" asked Merton.

"Yes. A set arrived at my office a week ago Thursday. A letter accompanying the pictures said if I didn't put a million dollars—in small bills—in a certain locker at the High Meadow YMCA, another set of the same pictures would be sent to my mother with a request for even more money."

"You didn't pay up?" asked Vesba who was still looking at the pictures.

"No. I don't have a million dollars and I couldn't get a million dollars. I had no choice..."

"And now your mother's dead!" hissed Sylvia Arno, who until that moment had stood at the window, her eyes fixed on the garden below while her hands clenched and unclenched at her sides.

"Yes!" said Carl Jr. "Now my mother's dead!" He glared at the woman by the window. She turned and glared back.

"Well, I'd say this complicates things just a wee bit," said Vesba amiably.

"Why?" asked Carl Jr. "Do you think the blackmail and the murder are connected?"

Sylvia Arno groaned and turned back to the window.

"It certainly bears looking into," said Merton. "Do you have any idea who was blackmailing you, Mr. Weinrich?"

"No. I'm afraid I do not."

"We'll have to take the pictures with us and we'll need the letter and any other communications you've had from the blackmailer."

"Of course. I understand."

Merton turned to Sylvia Arno. "When did Mrs. Weinrich receive her package?"

"Wednesday afternoon. In the regular mail. It was a terrible shock."

"Did she say anything about what she planned to do?" he asked.

"Yes. She said she'd take care of it," said Sylvia Arno. "She didn't go into any more detail than that."

"She didn't contact you?" asked Merton turning to face Carl Jr.

"No. She did not."

"It says in this letter," interrupted Vesba, "that 'since your son Carl Weinrich, Jr. chose not to deal with us, we are forced to deal with you...'. It says they want $5 million for the negatives."

Sylvia Arno shook her head. "She would have taken care of it. She'd done it before. Someone just killed her before she had a chance to. I wonder if the blackmailer will come back to you now, Carl Jr.?"

"What?" said Carl Jr. wrenching his head around to face her. "How could?" He broke off, swallowing his words. His Teutonic face was bright red.

"Leona, why don't you take Ms. Arno outside and talk to her while Mr. Weinrich and I go through the rest of the contents of the safe."

"Fine," said Vesba nodding at the secretary. "We'll talk somewhere else."

Sylvia flashed a look at Carl Jr., then shrugging, followed Vesba out of the room.

Merton sat down on the edge of the desk and fingered the yellow envelope. "What did Ms. Arno mean, Mr. Weinrich? What did she mean when she said your mother had taken care of things 'before'?"

Carl Jr. folded his arms and stood, feet apart, at the French window. Leaves blew against the window and skimmed back across the patio. "It means, Detective, that the acorn doesn't fall very far from the tree."

"Was your father blackmailed?"

"I really don't know about that. I do know that he was a skirt-chaser and that when my mother found out that he had cheated on her she moved him out of her bedroom to another bedroom down the hall. She explained to me when I was still quite young why I was an only child. I suppose she wanted to turn me against my father, but the effect was precisely the opposite. I wanted to be just like him. And in that one respect I have succeeded."

"Have you been blackmailed before?"

"Once. A long time ago. My mother took care of it."

"Was Ms. Arno here then?"

"Yes. She's been with my mother for 15 years or more—the

best years of *her* life."

"What does that mean?"

"Nothing," he said quickly. "It's just that she devoted herself to my mother—I don't think she's had any outside interests or friends."

"Does she live here?"

"Yes."

The detective wrote something down in his notebook. "Mr. Weinrich, who would have stood to benefit the most from your mother's death—monetarily, that is?"

"I would—as her only child. There are trust funds for my three children. She left some money to the Botanical Garden—too much if you ask me, but the director has had his hand out for years. She made him what he is today. Then there's the University, the Salvation Army...The church has never been in as far as I know. She'd changed her will a long time ago—some disagreement with God. The National Church as well, and she despised the bishop. I suppose he'll conduct the service though. I should get on the horn and arrange that..."

"And the school?" asked Merton.

"She took the school out of her will several years ago when it merged with Bingham Country Day. As far as I know she never changed that. God knows Buzz Pinchot's been working on it ever since he stepped foot in the state! Maybe he succeeded in convincing her; I've heard he's real good at his job. I just don't know."

"What about Ms. Arno?"

"Sylvia? Well, I suppose she'll get something. I really don't recall the details." Carl Jr. looked sideways at the safe for a few moments and then, turning from the window, said, "Let's take a look in that safe, shall we?" He walked quickly to the wall and reached inside. "Here's her life insurance policy—paid up years ago—some jewelry, a list of stocks, bonds...some cash...some notebooks..."

"May I see those please?" asked the detective reaching forward. Carl Jr. obligingly handed them to him and stepped back to the safe.

"Here are some photographs. Let me see...portrait proofs of her cocker, Oberon. Oh, how she loved that dog! *'My Oberon!'* she'd say. *'What visions have I seen! Methought I was enamoured of an ass!'* Meaning my father, of course... She grieved for that dog like she never grieved for my father."

Merton smiled. "These notebooks," he said, sitting now at

the desk. "They seem to be logs of...of hurts and insults...and paybacks..."

"Let me see," said Carl Jr. striding to the desk. He picked up a notebook randomly and scanned a page. *"March 1967: Harriet Fletcher: intimated that my admiration for the Tijuana Brass was plebian. Laughed at me. Asked if I had Spanish blood. September 1967: Application for membership in the Women's Forum denied...* For Christ's sake, they go on and on. She was systematic...Positively systematic..." He put the notebook down on the desk and shrugged his shoulders. "I had no idea, truly, not a clue! People—most people—seemed wary of her, but I always attributed that to her wealth." He paused, studying the view out the French window again.

"Did your mother have *any* friends?" asked Merton quickly.

"Yes, she did. Quite a few actually."

The detective pulled his notebook over. "Go ahead, please. I'll write down their names."

"Okay. Sure. She knew everybody, of course, at the Middle Essex Club, but her best friends were Ruth Travilla and Carol Selby and Peggy Warren. They've played bridge together every week for 50 years. More maybe. Those three I know for sure..."

"Thanks. That's enough to start with," said Merton. "That's helpful. I'd like to take these books if that's all right." Carl Jr. nodded. "We'll need to see a copy of the will as well."

"Yes, I'm surprised there isn't one in here now." Carl Jr. pointed to the safe. "I suppose she was working on it again. You'll have to check with David Whittier."

"Tell me, sir," began Merton as he picked up his notebook and pen and put them back in his pocket. "Where were you last night?"

Carl Jr. stuffed his hands in his pockets and flexed his knees. "I was at the Club—the Middle Essex Club—for dinner. I stayed for some drinks and got home around 11 o'clock."

"Can anyone confirm that?"

"Sure. Watson, the steward, and Toby Grove. I ate dinner with Toby. We're both batching it while our wives enjoy warmer climes. Willis McHugh was going to join us, but he had something else to do. So I was with Toby most of the night, but lots of people saw me. You can check."

"We will."

"I didn't kill my own mother."

Merton picked up the stack of black notebooks. He paused,

studying the other man's flushed face. "What was your mother's relationship with Renzi Stark?"

"Renzi? I don't think they had a 'relationship'."

"They both served on the board of the Rochester-Bingham School."

"So? That doesn't mean anything, Detective. Renzi's a junior attorney at my law firm. He's not even a partner yet—may never be. He's hardly on a level with my mother."

"We've been told that your mother threatened him over a board issue. She wanted his support, and said he'd be fired if he failed to give it."

"Maybe she did. That was certainly her style. But she never spoke to me about it."

"Would you have fired Renzi Stark if your mother had told you to?"

"Sure," said Carl Jr. crossing his arms. "I never crossed my mother—certainly not I if I could avoid it."

Chapter 9

It was an orange and yellow world in Ethel Weinrich's expansive, sloping backyard. Leaves from a hundred oak trees carpeted the lawn, entirely covering the grass, and yet, the trees themselves still seemed to hold on to most of their leaves. How typical, thought Vesba. Even the damn trees wouldn't let go of that which they considered their own. The breeze blew and the trees whispered, "Mine. Mine. Mine."

"We can sit over here if you'd like," said Sylvia Arno, indicating a low stone wall which ran around the patio. The two women sat down.

"This must be very hard for you," said Vesba. "I understand, but I have to ask you some questions." The other woman nodded and lowered her eyes to the hands in her lap. "How long did you work for Mr. Weinrich?"

"It's been fifteen, almost sixteen years," Sylvia replied as her face dissolved into a frown. She took a handkerchief from her jacket pocket and blew her nose.

"Did you enjoy your work?"

"Yes," she said as she squared her shoulders and stuffed the handkerchief back into her pocket. "It was good work...in a pleasant environment."

"Where did you work before?"

"I worked at Whittier, Weinrich and Goblenz as a paralegal."

"Oh?" said the detective. She leaned out from the wall but could not catch the other woman's eye. "Whose idea was the move to the...home office?"

"Mr. Weinrich—Carl Jr.—thought I might be a help, a good secretary for his mother. I tried to be of assistance in whatever capacity she needed."

"Meaning what exactly?"

"Meaning I was flexible. Since I lived here at the house, my job was not always 9 to 5. Sometimes I put together a meal if the cook was out or something like that. I was flexible. I didn't mind. She was always kind to me...and treated me like a..."

"Like a what?" prompted the detective.

"Like a friend, a companion. She confided in me. I think she trusted me."

"What kind of things did she tell you?"

"Oh, she talked about the different projects she was working on—civic projects and her volunteer work—and she told me about the people she worked with, her friends and...other people."

"Did she talk to you about the school, about the plan for a park there?"

"Of course," said Sylvia, brushing imaginary lint off her skirt. Her nails, Vesba noted, were beautifully manicured and painted a deep red color which contrasted disturbingly with the rest of her old-maidish façade. She wore no make-up, her graying hair was untouched and unimaginatively styled. Her suit, though well-tailored, made her look like a nun.

The detective blinked. "Did she mention anyone in particular?"

"Well, the headmaster, of course. She liked Buzz Pinchot. She thought he was a great improvement over Fred Twain, his predecessor. She didn't like that dean very much though—that Crabtree person. She hated the way he lorded his eastern prep school background over everyone and treated them like Midwestern hayseeds. She always wondered why in the world he ever came out here. She felt he must be running from something, some scandal, an affair or some such thing. Given time she probably would have found out what it was."

"Then what?"

"She would have ruined him."

"Ruined him? She could do that?"

"Of course. She was a powerful woman. You just didn't look down your nose at Ethel Weinrich and get away with it."

"Anyone else?" asked Vesba. "How about Renzi Stark?"

"Renzi Stark?" repeated Sylvia as she looked away.

"Yes. They were on the board together. We hear she threatened him. Said if he didn't support her on the park deal, he'd lose his job."

"Oh," said Sylvia, tossing her right hand up in a gesture of dismissal. "Threatening people was just a reflex with her...She didn't *always* mean anything by it."

"But most the time?" asked Vesba.

"Most of the time she meant it." Sylvia almost smiled, but reconsidered. "Actually I think she had a bit of a soft spot for Renzi. He loved the school, he respected the traditions, and that gave them a certain bond. He respected her too, you know, gave her her due. Not everyone did."

Vesba smiled, but Sylvia Arno did not. The detective imagined that she did not smile often. "What about you, Ms. Arno? Did she ever threaten you?"

Sylvia Arno regarded the detective thoughtfully. "No. Not that I can remember. We got along well. I understood her."

"You mean you knew how to handle her?"

"Yes."

Vesba re-crossed her fat legs and referred to her notebook. "There's one thing I've been wondering about. How was Mrs. Weinrich supposed to get home last night? Was someone going to drive her home? There was no car found at the school."

Sylvia turned her narrow face to the detective. "Mrs. Weinrich employs a full-time chauffeur who drives her everywhere. Last night, for some reason, she gave Mr. Ryan, the chauffeur, the night off. I believe she planned to ask Renzi Stark to drive her home. She had done that before."

"And didn't you notice when she failed to return?"

"No. I'm afraid I didn't."

"And where were you last night, Ms. Arno?"

"I was here, of course."

"Doing what?"

"As a matter of fact I was in the kitchen. I made my dinner, and lots of people saw me in the kitchen. The cook, Mrs. Brauer, for instance and Dorothy, the maid who lives downstairs. I ate in the kitchen and then I went up to my rooms. I went to bed at 9:30 and fell asleep reading. I'm a sound sleeper. I didn't know a thing about any of this until Mr. Weinrich called me this morning."

Chapter 10

It was amazing what you could see if you just sat still. Page Hawthorne reclined on a wooden chaise on the patio behind her house. She squinted at the sky, its perfect emptiness interrupted in the space of five minutes by an array of flying objects, including three airplanes, a butterfly, a crow, several insects. A gray squirrel inspected the empty birdbath, barely aware of her presence. An intermittent south-easterly breeze rustled the leaves, saying, *Glory to God, Glory to God.*

Page looked around at the summer detritus: an overturned ice chest, a half-full bag of potting soil, a trowel, two empty flower pots, and three popsicle sticks on the ground. It was time she knew for everything to be put away. It was time to clean up and stack the chairs and cover the grill. She did not move. The breeze said *Glory to God.*

The back of her house was plain brick, the windows unadorned rectangles without shutters. There was a light by the back door and a flower box at the kitchen window, still spilling over with white impatiens. Page loved her unremarkable house, and she loved the things inside it: her books and music, her highboy and her needlework, and her boys. It was enough. She didn't miss her job, which she had given up after last October's horror—the murder of a priest at the church where she worked, followed by two more murders and the resignation of the rector. The Rev. Charles Pinkney and his wife had moved as far away as possible from Middle Essex, to California and a small, but growing parish in a largely Hispanic neighborhood. They seemed to be happy. Charles had invited her to move with him, offering her a job, but she had stayed, maintaining that her sons needed stability. Everyone thought they knew what she really meant she needed was that detective, the one who had broken the case and saved her life. But she had shut them up when she broke up with him in the spring. Since then no one had talked much about her.

She caught herself thinking about the detective and she opened her eyes. She hopped off the chaise and picked up a rubber bucket. She looked around for the popsicle sticks and bent to pick them up. She picked up the flowerpots and they followed the popsicle sticks into the bucket. Presently she caught the edge of a sound, a young voice shrill and exuberant. They would be rounding the corner and coming into the cul de sac. She dumped the bucket and walked around the house, kicking leaves noisily, enjoying the sound. She looked up. They had just started up the front walk. "Hey you!" she called.

"Mom!" cried the smaller of the two boys, bounding forward, leaving the older boy behind.

"Hey, Tal," said Page as she absorbed the energy of the seven-year old projectile that leapt into her arms. "How was your day?"

"Fine," said Tal leaning back, but still hanging on. "Can I get something to eat?"

"Yes. Of course." She smiled and turned to Walter, her older son who had slowly come up the walk. "How was *your* day, dear?" she asked as she ruffled his hair.

He turned away, smoothing his hair. "Just fine. I got 100% on my math test. The DARE officer talked to my class about sniffing household chemicals, and Derek Washington got a lunch detention and cried. How was your day?"

Page put her arm around him and they walked together to the front door. "My day was fine too. I read a short story by Rex Stout and made a meatloaf for dinner. I missed you."

"I missed you too, Mom." He stopped. "Did you talk to anyone today? Did you go out?"

"No, I didn't," she said, crossing her arms. "I waved to Mr. Lindgren across the street. Does that count?"

"No," said Walter. "It does not count."

LEAVEN OF MALICE

Chapter 11

The law firm of Whittier, Weinrich and Goblenz took up the top two floors of the Metropolitan Building downtown. David Whittier's office was located in the northeast corner of the top floor and commanded a dramatic view of the river. His assistant ushered the detectives in and announced them. David Whittier stood up and greeted them, pumping their hands in an unexpectedly affectionate manner. His gentle smile reflected just the right amount of sorrow, sympathy and willingness to help. "I'm sorry to see you again under these circumstances, Roy, but it is a pleasure nonetheless," he said.

Vesba's eyes flashed a question at her partner.

"Mr. Whittier is Page Hawthorne's godfather," explained Merton. "We met once before."

Vesba puckered her lips and inhaled loudly, nodding.

The assistant left, walking backwards, and they all sat down. After a moment David Whittier leaned forward and said, "Carl Jr. called this morning and told me what has happened. I've heard from Buzz Pinchot as well. Please tell me what I can do to help you." His eagerness was genuine and, therefore, charming, and the detectives relaxed.

"Thank you, sir," said Merton as he felt inside his jacket for his notebook. "We were wondering if…"

"Ethel Weinrich dead!" interrupted Whittier, slapping the arms of his leather desk chair for emphasis and shattering the calm atmosphere. His eyes were suddenly round and wide with indignation. "Murdered! The old gal seemed so…so indestructible. Why it was only this past Tuesday that she came in to see me. We had lunch as always at the Noonday Club—she had a chicken sandwich, white meat only, with mayonnaise, no lettuce, on white bread, just as she always had. Iced tea—lemon only; potato chips—

no ridges. Christ, Ethel never changed a thing about her routine. The only thing she ever changed was her will! Her magnus opus, her life's work..." Whittier's shoulders began to shake and he pressed his eyes shut, shielding them with one hand.

Merton, concentrating hard on the other man, could not tell if the attorney was laughing or crying or merely trying to control himself. He waited for him to continue as Vesba stared at her own hands clasped in her lap. After a respectable interlude, Merton finally cleared his throat and said, "Actually, Sir, that is exactly what we wanted to talk to you about."

"I see...Ethel's will," said Whittier, calm again. "She came in Tuesday to make some changes," said Whittier. He reached across the desk and picked up a 17" x 8 ½" folder. "That was not at all unusual. She did that on a regular basis. She was an attorney herself, you know, one of the first female graduates of the University law school."

"What changes did she make this week?" asked Merton reaching for the folder.

"This week," said the attorney, holding on to the folder. "She made a few minor personal adjustments, and then..." He paused for effect, still holding on to the folder as Merton's arm remained poised over the desk. "This week Ethel made a big change. She put the Rochester-Bingham School back in her will as a beneficiary. As the will reads now the school stands to receive $20 million."

The heads of both men jerked in the direction of Vesba as she let out a long, shrill whistle. She smiled serenely when she was finished and said, "Well, gentlemen, the $64,000 question now is: Who knew about the will being changed? Who the hell knew?"

"Well, *no* one, Detective," said Whittier, releasing the folder into Roy's outstretched hand. "Except me and..."

"And anyone Ethel chose to tell?" finished Merton.

"And who would she have told?" asked Vesba.

"I have no idea," said Whittier.

"How about her secretary? Sylvia Arno?" asked Merton.

"She might have," said the attorney. "But I don't think you quite grasp the situation. You see, Ethel changed her will all the time. Back and forth. You're in, you're out. If she hadn't died, she might very well have taken the school right back out..."

"Exactly," said Vesba folding her arms and smiling like a contented cat. "Bingo."

Whittier gawked at her for several seconds. "Detective,

please. If you are implying that anyone connected with the Rochester-Bingham School might have been involved, I can assure you that such an idea is preposterous..."

"You can't assure me of any such thing," said Vesba evenly. "Money makes people do crazy things. It turns them into reckless idiots..."

The attorney waved his hand at the detectives and dropped it like a stone on to his desk. "Reckless *idiots!* Whoever killed Ethel Weinrich was no reckless idiot. No. It was someone who planned carefully and blind-sided her. Ethel was no everyday, garden-variety *victim.*" He stopped suddenly and looked at his fist on his desk. He opened it slowly as if hoping to find something there. He sighed, finding it empty, and raised his eyes to the two detectives. He searched their faces. "You don't seem to understand, Detectives. The School didn't *need* Ethel's twenty million dollars. Not really. Not in such a way as to motivate someone to kill...to murder Ethel. There's always someone else waiting to be asked for money, someone who wants more than anything to have a building named after him."

"So you think this change in the will is just a coincidence?" asked Merton.

"Yes, I do," said the attorney. "Ethel was a hard woman, a difficult woman, but she didn't deserve to die this way. Not for *money*...not for her money."

Chapter 12

Renzi Stark was not a big man. He was tall, but slightly built with narrow shoulders. It was hard to imagine him playing football, even for an ABC League private school. Merton eyed him critically as he stood with his partner in the man's small, dark-paneled office on the floor below David Whittier.

"Have a seat, Detectives," he said indicating the two client chairs which barely fit in front of his large desk. "It's no corner office, but at least I've got a window," he said grinning. "What can I do for you?"

"Perhaps you haven't heard," said Merton. "Ethel Weinrich was found this morning, deceased."

"Ethel? Deceased?" asked Renzi Stark, the color draining from his face as his hand moved slowly to his neck and loosened his tie. "Ethel Weinrich?"

"Yes," said Merton, pausing a moment to allow the other man to regain his evaporating composure. "When was the last time you saw her?"

"The last time?" stammered Stark. He took a deep breath and placed his hands palms down on the desk in front of him. "She was at the board meeting last night at the school—the Rochester-Bingham School. She sat across from me in the Blankenship Room. She looked good. I mean she hadn't been feeling well the month before, but she looked better, I thought, healthier. That's not to say that she was in good spirits, however. She was giving them hell about the park, the park she wanted to build...the trees...and all. She left in a huff. She was all worked up over something George Crabtree said...some crack about Johnny Appleseed..."

"Did you follow her out?" asked Merton.

"Yes," said the other man who had risen abruptly and

stepped to the credenza where he poured himself a glass of water with hands that shook. He drank down the water quickly. "I could tell she was upset. I thought someone should follow her, and no one else seemed to be inclined that way."

"And..." prompted Vesba who leaned forward to get a better look at something on his desk.

"And so I did and I asked her if she was all right," he said turning back to his desk. She gave me one of her withering looks and said, 'Oh leave me alone, Renzi, for god's sake.' That was all. She didn't want sympathy. I left her alone."

"Did you go straight back to the boardroom?" asked Merton.

"No. I went around the corner and called my wife on my cell phone. One of our kids was sick, nothing serious, but I wanted to check, you know."

"Is this your wife?" asked Vesba picking up a framed photograph from the desktop.

"Yes. That's Augusta and our two children: Nicholas and Jane. Janie had a sore throat—nothing serious, you know, but I wanted to make sure she was okay."

"Your family is beautiful," she said meaning it. She replaced the photo on the desk after showing it to her partner.

"Did you see anyone or hear anything while you were in the hall?" Merton asked.

"No, I...I wasn't paying attention," said Stark as he sat back down at his desk. "We were running late and I wanted to tell Augusta. I don't understand all this. Where was she...where did you find Ethel?"

"In the cafeteria," said Merton.

"*At the school?*" asked Stark, his face becoming even paler. He stood up again. He sat down.

"At the school," repeated Merton. "She may have been poisoned."

"Oh good God," said Stark lowering his eyes to his hands. Then he looked up slowly as a thought apparently occurred to him. "You're saying she was murdered? Murdered at the school?"

"Yes."

"Do you think this had anything to do with the building? Could someone have...could someone have *killed her over the trees?*"

"It's an idea to consider," said Merton evenly. "We've heard that Mrs. Weinrich threatened you—your job was at stake if you didn't support her."

Stark's eyes were round blue discs in his face. Then suddenly the corners of his mouth pulled back and he said, "Oh, I never took anything she said like that seriously. She wasn't really going to do anything about that. No. I never gave it a second thought."

"Is that so?" said Vesba as she leaned forward allowing her pendulous breasts to rest on her knees, her substantial cleavage in full view of the attorney.

Stark did not blink or look down, but leaned forward slightly himself. "No, Detective, I never did."

"It didn't bother you when she said that your opinion was irrelevant because you yourself were not relevant?" she asked.

Stark sighed. "Sure it bothered me...for a little while. But I've been around these people long enough to know that I'm not going to change any of them. I'm not going to teach them manners or make them care. All I can do is be Renzi Stark and hope that some day somebody will say at my funeral, 'Yeah, Renzi Stark was okay. He never called anyone names or cheated.'"

"Or murdered anyone?" asked Vesba.

"Exactly," said Stark calmly. "Renzi Stark never murdered anyone..." He smiled, but his eyes held no mirth.

Vesba sat up straight again and referred to her notebook. "Well, then, Mr. Stark, answer me this. Were you planning to drive Mrs. Weinrich home last night after the board meeting?"

"No," he said moving his head slightly from left to right and back again.

"She never asked you to drive her home?"

"Not last night. She had on one other occasion I can remember, but not last night. Why do you ask?"

"Mrs. Weinrich's secretary said that Mrs. Weinrich had given the chauffeur the night off. She said she thought that Mrs. W. was planning to get a ride with you."

Stark blinked several times. "Why would she say that I wonder?"

"Yes, why?" repeated Vesba.

"It makes no sense, because Ethel wouldn't have just come to the meeting without a ride home like some high school kid. That's why she had a secretary to take care of things. She really was a great lady, you know, and she did things the old-fashioned way. If she had needed a ride home, her secretary would have called my secretary well ahead of time and arranged things."

"I see," said Merton.

"That could be significant, I suppose," mused Stark.

"Or totally insignificant," said Vesba. "We'll follow it up. That's what we do."

Stark nodded. "How...how did you say she was killed?"

"That has not been established. We think she was poisoned," said Merton.

"This makes no sense, because...You must think it was someone she knew...and trusted?" he said. The detectives nodded. "How ghastly for her. How awful." He looked away as his eyes filled with tears.

"Yes," agreed Merton. "Whoever killed Ethel Weinrich, looked her right in the eye as he did it."

Chapter 13

Vesba maneuvered through the maze of desks back to her own and set down a cup of coffee. She handed a second cup to her partner who looked up absent-mindedly and murmured thanks. She sat down across from him and pulled a bound, black ledger-type book towards her. "I've seen plenty of strange things in my years on the force, but *never* anything quite like this," she said.

Merton expelled a short nasal report in agreement, but did not look up.

"I've got over 100 different names already, Roy—all paid back with interest for having the nerve to make a vaguely unflattering comment pertaining to a new hairdo in 1964 or for not responding s'il vous plait to an invitation in 1957—or worse—responding positively and then not showing up to a New Year's Eve party in 1970. Do you really think any of these names will lead us anywhere but to the conclusion that Ethel Weinrich was an obsessive, compulsive, neurotic nut case?"

"Maybe not, but the computer boys can play with our notes and—who knows? We could get lucky." He looked up then as his partner stretched, arching her back and groaning in a burlesque of bona fide fatigue. He smiled. "Leona, why don't you go home? I'll finish up here—you go home to Valerie. I bet she's cooking up something special, just for you."

"Hmm," she murmured. "I could relate to a big bowl of hot pesto right about now." She opened her eyes suddenly and said, "Not to mention the fact that you've been driving me crazy for the past hour with your humming. What the hell is that anyway?"

Merton smiled. "What's what?"

"That tune, that annoying tune!"

"Just an old Johnny Cash song—*No eye for an eye/ no tooth for a tooth/ I see Judas Iscariot carrying John Wilkes Booth/ Down there by the train..."*

"I'm sorry I asked," said Vesba. She reached for the bottom drawer where she kept her purse. She extracted it noisily and set it in her lap. She pulled out a hand mirror and fluffed her hair. "Hey, Roy, you never told me. How do you like me as a blond?"

Merton's eyebrows shot up and he considered her for a moment, formulating a reply. She put down the mirror and gaped at him. "Didn't you even notice? I've been a blond—Tahitian Blond—now for five whole days!"

"I like it," he said nodding. "I liked the red too..."

"Bull shit," Vesba said acidly. She pulled out a bulging cosmetics bag and selected a lipstick. She flicked open her compact mirror again and began to apply a new coat of gleaming, frosted paste. She pressed her lips together as she closed the bag with a snap.

"I guess it's more to the point to ask what Jerry thinks," said Merton.

Vesba narrowed her eyes at him. "Jerry loves it." She stood up and kicked the drawer closed with a bang. "I'm out of here."

"Is Jerry working late?"

"Yes, he is," she said, throwing her jacket around her shoulders. "I'm going home to my darling daughter who is grounded." She paused. "Don't stay here all night, okay? Go rustle up some action."

"Go home."

She paused again. "I'm serious. What are you going to do?"

"I'm going to finish up here."

"And then what?"

"Don't worry, Leona. I won't be here all night. I've got an eBay auction ending in a couple of hours."

She stared. "My ass."

He blinked. "I'm watching an 1898 Rolfe *Macbeth*."

"I see," she said. She leveled one more look at him, then turned on her three-inch heels and beat a flamboyant tattoo to the door where she turned back to her partner. "And get that humming crap out of your system for god's sake if you expect me to come back tomorrow."

She was gone and the office was empty and silent. It always seemed to him as if Leona breathed more than her share of the air in a room, so when she left, the difference was noticeable. He acknowledged that she was well-meaning and motivated by brotherly love, but he wished she would back off. He knew he shouldn't tease her. He leaned back in his chair and surveyed his desktop. Then he sat forward in his chair, his arms resting on the desk, and stared at the assembled notebooks. He knew what it felt like to be empty and indifferent. But what was it, he wondered, that could turn a woman into the paranoid, vengeance-seeking witch Mrs. Weinrich appeared to have been? Why the compulsion to avenge herself, to get even and pay back even the smallest slights? Why had those slights loomed so large in her eyes? Was the person who killed Ethel Weinrich someone who had suffered as a victim of her revenge? His instincts said no, this was a private war Mrs. Weinrich had waged. It was something she did for her own peace of mind. She was only being fair, after all, and doing unto others as they had done to her.

He sighed, and conceding that this was no doubt an unmitigated exercise in futility leading nowhere, turned to the notebook in front of him and opened it.

Chapter 14

Carol Selby lived in the penthouse of one of the high rise buildings overlooking the Park on Hitchcock Boulevard. A servant let them in, invited them to wait in the spacious living room, and then disappeared. The view was reminiscent of Central Park from the West Side of New York City, but only vaguely. The apartment was spacious with high ceilings, expensively decorated with tasteful arrangements of real flowers and family pictures in silver frames. There were bookshelves on either side of the fireplace filled with books that looked liked they might actually have been read. Merton checked out their titles, while Vesba leaned on a large desk and scrutinized her pocket calendar.

She kept them waiting twenty minutes. They knew it was an action specifically intended to put them in their place, and she knew they knew it. Ten minutes meant a person was running late, sorry for the inconvenience. Twenty minutes meant you are beneath my notice; you can wait. When she did arrive, Mrs. Selby glided into her living room and stood by the fireplace, her chin lifted, her hands clasped. Detectives," she said, not bothering to mask her contempt.

Merton, wearing a suit which smelled only slightly of mothballs, stepped toward her, offering his hand. She ignored it. He smiled as he lowered it. "How do you do, ma'am?" he asked.

"Let's dispense with the country niceties, shall we?" she snapped. "I haven't much time for you two, so ask me what you want to ask me and go."

"That suits us fine," said Vesba stepping forward in reaction to the perceived aggression of Selby. She took a deep breath. "May we sit down?"

"By all means, Detective. Take a load, as they say in your

part of town, off your feet."

Vesba and her partner lowered themselves carefully into matching wing chairs as if they suspected booby-trapping. Carol Selby remained standing and noted the time on her wristwatch. Vesba slowly opened her vinyl handbag and extracted her spiral notebook. Then she fished around noisily for a pen.

Merton crossed his long legs and relaxed, content to let his partner take the lead in the interview. He gazed at Mrs. Selby as if fascinated while inwardly practicing glottal constriction. She was, he had to admit, an elegant woman, but she was overly proud of her trim figure, her straight spine, her abundant ash blond hair, worn in a French twist. She wore a silk pantsuit in a flattering lavender shade and matching shoes. Her jewelry was gold, no doubt custom designed. She sighed and walked to the window.

"So, ma'am," said Vesba, having at last located a writing utensil. "Could you tell us about your friend Ethel Weinrich?"

"She was my friend," said Mrs. Selby, lacing her fingers. "Our relationship reflected most aspects implied in the word *friend*."

"You played bridge?" asked Vesba, ignoring the sarcasm.

"Yes."

"You talked to each other while you played?"

"Yes."

"What did you talk about?"

Carol Selby sighed again and turned around. She folded her arms and looked at the detectives as if they were large and particularly distasteful apes. "Lots of things. Everything! What friends talk about—other people."

"What other people?" said Vesba.

"Well, I don't know," she stammered. "Monday night we talked about the controversy at the school—the Rochester-Bingham School. Ethel was livid about the new building which she saw, and rightly so, as a bridge between the two schools. She had never recovered, really, from the merger—that merger which had been accomplished when she was on a European tour, when she was out of the country!"

"She was opposed to the merger? Was she on the board then?" asked Vesba.

"Yes. She didn't think anything would happen while she was gone, but that trip was engineered for the specific purpose of getting her out of the way. She never got over that treachery."

"Perpetrated by whom?" asked Merton.

"Perpetrated by the then headmaster of Rochester Hall, Fred Twain, and Bradford Cole. He was the President of the Rochestser Board then."

Vesba glanced at her partner who continued to stare at his tented fingers.

"She was on a tour of European botanical gardens with Ben Bodine, the director of our local Botanical Garden. I always suspected he was involved somehow, paid off by Cole, but it could never be proven." Carol Selby began to pace. "He's damn lucky Ethel never thought so or that huge planned gift the Garden will receive now wouldn't be his."

"No?" asked Vesba innocently.

"No. Ethel loved to change her will. She was a lawyer herself, you know, one of the first women graduates of the University Law School. She changed her will herself several times a year."

"Really?" said Vesba, making a notation.

"Really. She had taken Rochester Hall out of her will when the merger took place. To my knowledge she never put it back, but what do I really know? Ethel was a contradictory woman in many ways. To a lot of people I'm sure she appeared to be cold and self-controlled and ruthless, when really, she was like so many women locked into unsatisfactory, loveless marriages. She craved attention and was therefore so easily influenced by the attentions of a certain type of man." She stopped her pacing and leveled her cold pale eyes at Merton, attempting to skewer him. He resisted, leveling his own wide gaze at her. "You know the type, Detective. The type who preys on the lonely, sexually-repressed widow or divorcee. The type who does so well in the development field and working for not-for-profit agencies."

He arched an eyebrow, but did not respond verbally. Vesba pinched herself and said, "Do you two know each other?"

Mrs. Selby unburdened herself of a laugh and turned back to the window. "Of course not. But I heard all about you last year. I suppose you two wonder why you didn't get promotions after those Holy Comforter murders. Such a high-profile case, such a dramatic finale...But I suspect Mayor McHugh didn't appreciate the fact that one of you was sleeping with his cousin's wife, and the other killed the poor cuckolded fool."

Merton rose to his feet and took a step towards the old woman. "Chester Hawthorne may have been a fool, but he was never cuckolded, certainly not by his *ex*-wife. He was a *murderer*, ma'am

...three times over."

She stepped back but thrust her jaw defiantly forward. "Details," she said waving her hand through the air as if dispelling irritating insects. "The point I was endeavoring to make, Detective, is that Willis McHugh's mother was Ethel's cousin. Did you know that?"

"I may have noticed a certain family resemblance."

"More than that, Detective. Ethel hand-picked Willis to succeed her as mayor of Middle Essex."

"And how did that turn out, ma'am? Was she pleased with her cousin's turn as mayor?"

Carol Selby waved her hand dismissively through the air again. "That is hardly pertinent here. But I do have a word of warning for you, Detectives. Mayor McHugh—like Ethel Weinrich—never forgets a wrong done him."

"Well, I never knew you cared," said Vesba, as she stood up with some effort, both knees cracking.

Mrs. Selby colored slightly and turned away. "You think you're witty, Detective," she said. "But you are merely vulgar, coming here into my home, which I cultivate as a sanctuary in this tawdry world, and asking your cold questions about my dearest friend." She turned back, steadying herself with a hand on the mantel. "Ethel may not have been perfect, but she strove for perfection. She wanted Middle Essex to be perfect, a perfect jewel of refinement in a spoiled and decadent world. You two exemplify what she hated in the modern world."

Vesba planted her feet further apart and folded her hands over her protruding abdomen. "Oh, really?" she asked. "Perhaps you'd like to..."

"Did you know, Mrs. Selby," interrupted Merton, "that Ethel Weinrich kept log books of personal insults and lists of how she paid people back?"

He thought he saw her shoulders tense, but she did not turn around. "No, I didn't, not specifically. I knew she was very keen on justice being done and on making sure people got what they deserved."

"Why?" asked Vesba. "Why was she so keen on that?"

"Well," said Selby, suddenly wistful. "I suppose she never felt she got what she deserved. Not really."

"Well, maybe she finally did," mumbled Vesba.

"We're finished here I think," said Merton quickly as Mrs.

Selby turned to face Vesba.

"Yes," she said weakly as she turned away again. "I want you both to leave immediately."

Vesba snapped her mouth shut on a reply and she moved to the door.

"Have a nice day, Mrs. Selby," said Merton staring at the old lady's straight back.

"Mayor McHugh will hear about your rudeness," she hissed. "You can count on that." She waited, clinging to the mantel with arthritic fingers, and did not turn around until she heard the front door close.

Chapter 15

"Bitch!" said Vesba slapping the steering wheel for effect as she turned to look at her partner. "What was all that about?"

"All what about?" asked Merton calmly.

"Oh, nothing. She just said we exemplified all that was filthy in the world. Jesus, she practically called you a whore! Why'd you sit still for that?"

"I didn't sit still," he said. "I stood up."

"Oh, shit," said Vesba slapping the steering wheel once again. "You know what I mean."

"What was I going to do, Leona? I corrected her, but people are entitled to their opinions."

"Yeah, well, I just don't understand where these rich old broads like her get off thinking they can say whatever they think anytime they think it. Like calling that Renzi Stark irrelevant and us ...well, I mean everyone's got an opinion. Jesus, you might as well be dead as not have opinions. But they think their opinions are so freaking important, like we're supposed to care. I would just like someone to explain to me who made her queen bee?"

"I think she was putting up a brave front. She's upset because her best friend of fifty years has been murdered."

Vesba sighed and lifted her shoulders. "And scared maybe. You're probably right. But you know, I believe her about one thing—she'll complain to McHugh."

"She's probably on the phone right now. Being able to do something will make her feel better." Merton looked straight forward through the windshield. "It's unsettling, I have to admit."

"What's unsettling?"

"Revisiting Babylon."

Vesba followed his gaze down the street where a few blocks

away the limestone edifice of the Episcopal Church of the Holy Comforter stood. A mere twelve months earlier they had investigated the murder of a priest at the church. It was there that her partner had met Page Hawthorne. He had been happy for awhile while she recovered from the wounds her crazy ex-husband had inflicted on her. In fact, he had practically moved in with her, driving her sons around while she couldn't and watching those stupid old movies they liked. He had even told Vesba, in a moment of unprecedented self-revelation, that it was the first time he had ever been 'friends' with a woman. Vesba had asked him what *she* was, and he had said 'his partner,' and closed down the conversation for good. Of course, he meant that he had gotten to know Page as a person before he slept with her, a first, no doubt, for him. But he had convinced himself he was in love and even asked her to marry him, the misguided pinhead. She had turned him down, and he had taken it hard. Not that he had discussed any of that with Vesba.

She shivered and started the engine abruptly. "Unsettling my ass," she said.

Chapter 16

Although it was autumn, the temperatures still soared in the Midwest, and sprinklers slapped the Rockville lawns in a lazy, haphazard fashion. From the bleachers Page gazed at the soccer field, only half watching Walter's fifth grade team warm up. Walter was pretty good, she thought, actually better than pretty good. She could take no credit for his athletic ability. No, in that, he took after his father.

She sighed, thinking of last year's soccer games, when, week after week, Walter would look for his father who never came to watch. He couldn't come this year. He was dead. She looked around at the other parents. A few looked familiar, but she didn't know them well. No one looked at her. After all, she was the one whose ex-husband had murdered those three people last year. What kind of person would ever have been married to someone like that? She had made herself sit right behind two women she recognized as mothers of boys in Walter's class. They had glanced back and mumbled vague greetings to her. They had not moved. That was something.

She looked back at the players who were gathering now in two circles around two men. Walter's team raised their hands and shouted in unison. The game was about to start. "Page?" someone said in a thin, strident voice next to her. "Page Browning?"
Page turned her head reflexively and stared. Her brain struggled to catch up.

"Page! Do you remember me? Gussie Stark? Gussie *Watson* Stark?"

Page's mind reeled backwards over the years to high school. She hadn't changed much. Her hair was still long and dark and unruly. She still tried to tame it with a tortoiseshell headband. Page met her startled brown eyes and smiled. "Of course, I remember.

You haven't changed at all."

"I'm sorry to bother you here," said the woman, focusing on Page with alarming concentration. She spoke quickly, her voice charged with tension and suppressed emotion. "Do you have a child playing soccer?"

"Yes. Walter—Number 8 on the Tucker Tornadoes." She pointed to the field and in the general direction of her son who had just settled the ball and was attempting to take it down the field. "Do you?"

"Yes," said the other woman who did not move her eyes from Page. "My son Nick plays for the North Woodward Tidal Waves."

The crowd began to cheer and clap. Page turned to see the Tucker Tornadoes high-fiving each other and running to the center line. "Who scored?" she asked the woman in front of her.

The woman turned around and stared at Page. "Walter scored. Didn't you even see?"

"Oh, I'm so sorry, Page," said Gussie Stark in a voice that suggested imminent tears. She stared at the hands in her lap. "It's just that I'm upset about this whole Ethel Weinrich murder. Have you heard about this? She was killed during the Board of Trustees meeting on Thursday night. The detectives have even talked to Renzi, my husband."

"Oh, I see," said Page, struggling to connect the dots. "Well, let's talk after the game—We can go back to my house. It isn't far."

The other woman raised her troubled eyes to Page. "The boys can play. They'll like that."

Page tried to smile reassuringly at her old friend0. "Now we better pay attention to the game." She made a face at the woman in front of her and Gussie Stark pretended to laugh.

Chapter 17

"So what did Jerry figure out?"

"Didn't he tell you?" said Merton. He did not look up but continued to study the report in his hand.

"Val told me you called. Sorry I couldn't get back to you." Vesba drummed on her partner's desk with the gaily-painted nails of her left hand. She exhaled. "So was she poisoned?"

He nodded. "Prunus serotina," he said.

"In English, Professor."

Merton grinned and pushed the file across his desk to Vesba. "Black cherry seeds. They contain cyanogenic glycoside amygdalin, which yields hydrocyanic acid. When ingested it can lead to difficult breathing, paralysis of the voice, twitching, spasms, coma of short duration, and death."

"Pretty gruesome," said Leona closing the file folder. "I'd say it sounds like a woman."

"Why do you say that?"

"Because I can't picture any of the men in this picture donning an apron and baking up cherry tarts."

"I think you're taking a very narrow view of things."

"Yeah?" said Vesba squinting slightly. "Well, how about this? Maybe we should think about this cherry tart thing some more. I mean, why a tart? What does 'tart' mean anyway?"

"You mean besides the obvious 'small pie or pastry'?"

"Uh huh. What else does it mean?"

"Sour, as in the late Mrs. Weinrich," said Merton.

Vesba crossed her arms across her bosom and chuckled. "No, I mean how about 'prostitute'? Maybe someone was sending a message here…"

"*Leona,*" said Merton as he stretched his arms over his head.

He lowered them slowly. "You're really stretching now."

"Am I? There are ways to screw someone other than sexually."

Merton smiled. "You're right about that. Perhaps we should be taking a wider view."

"A wider view meaning exactly what?"

"Meaning we should maybe be looking for a team here," he said. "A team of killers. Killer musk oxen."

"Musk oxen?"

"They form a circle, heads to the middle, in order to protect one of their own."

Chapter 18

"Your house is nice, Page," said Augusta Stark. She looked around distractedly at the yard and at the three boys who kicked a soccer ball in a widening triangle beyond the patio where she and Page sat sipping mineral water.

"Thanks," said Page. "It is nice to be able to sit outside like this so late in the year. It's crazy."

"Yes. Crazy," said Augusta wanting to be agreeable.

"So tell me about Renzi," said Page, gazing at this woman she had not seen in years, putting her in context, attempting to focus and care.

"Renzi is a *suspect*...a suspect in Ethel Weinrich's murder." Gussie covered her mouth, as if saying those particular words had hurt her teeth.

Page looked at her old classmate and sensed desperation under the surface, fear under the skin. She wanted to take her hand, to say everything's all right, but plainly everything was not all right. She fought the urge to utter cliches. "The police talked to him?" she asked instead.

"Yes. They talked to everyone who had attended the board meeting. But it's the board itself—the whole board—that's got me scared. It's turning on Renzi, because he's not one of them, he's the odd man out. He's expendable."

Page sighed and waited for Gussie to continue. She knew vaguely that Renzi Stark had worked his way up the Alumni Association ladder until he was elected President, at last, and had a seat, therefore, on the Board of Trustees. As an appointed member, Renzi Stark was probably not, in the eyes of many, on an equal footing with the rest of the board.

"Renzi couldn't have done this, Page. They're crazy to

think...he would never *plan* anything like this. He was on the way out anyway. He had one year to go...He was looking forward to saying goodbye to all that...He'd learned his lesson."

"What do you mean, 'learned his lesson'?"

"Renzi's so naïve, you know. He *trusted* all those people he'd looked up to when he was at school—people's parents and people like Mrs. Weinrich. It was natural, but what did he know?" She leaned back in her chair. "His parents were such social climbers. They sent him out to the school solely, I think, so they could join the Parents' Association and rub shoulders with the rich and powerful. You know the type. They sent Renzi with nothing—no social graces, not even the right clothes, nothing—but he survived because he could do one thing as it turned out. He could play football. He played for four years. He would have been a total nonentity, ignored except for the ability to throw the ball. So he made friends and was invited to parties. Girls went out with him. He had an identity. He was happy. He believed the school *gave* him that and he was grateful. After college he was drawn back to the place where he had been happy. He willingly called at telethons every year until he was finally heading up Annual Giving. He would do all the jobs no one else wanted. Finally they had to elect him to Alumni Association office, starting with secretary, treasurer, second vice president, vice president. Finally he was the president, and he did all right for awhile..."

"Then what happened?"

"He just couldn't 'stay in the wheelbarrow' with Buzz Pinchot. He began to be the minority voice at board meetings—not to be obnoxious, but just to remind them that there is another side to every issue, to point out when they were particularly inconsistent or hypocritical."

"He and Buzz were at odds?"

"Not all the time. He liked Buzz at first. He approved wholeheartedly when they hired him. But Buzz sold out fast—it's part of the game. If you don't, they get you. He was in Kruppenheim's pocket."

"Kruppenheim is the board president?"

"Yes. He and Renzi got along okay for awhile, but..." he looked down at her hands and her shoulders began to shake very gently.

Page leaned forward. "I'm sure everything will be just fine, Gussie. The police will find out who killed Ethel Weinrich. Don't worry."

"How can I not worry?" said Augusta wiping her eyes with the back of her hand. "He was there, and they think he had a motive."

"What motive?"

"Ethel had threatened him—everyone on the board seems to have known about it. She said if he didn't support her in her ridiculous efforts to stop the construction of the new administration building, he'd be fired, he'd lose his job."

"His job?" Page's mind skipped back trying to remember what Renzi Stark did for a living.

"He's an attorney—with Whittier, Weinrich and Goblenz. Her son Carl Jr. is still the managing partner. But Renzi never took her threats seriously. His clients had no connection with the school. He never played that card. It never helped his career, being on the board, not like people assume. That isn't why Renzi worked for the Alumni Association. It wasn't to further his career, to make contacts. People just think that because that's why *they* do it—for networking. He just loved the school, the way it used to be. He was grateful and thought it was his duty to give back. They just thought he was a sucker for not taking advantage of the situation. Now he's going to be their stooge again."

"Does Renzi have any idea who might have had a real motive to kill her?"

"He says half the board was fed up with the way she was delaying the ground breaking of the new building. She was talking about getting her friends to lie down in front of the bulldozers if it came to that."

"They really took her seriously?"

"They had to...with all that money. Now Renzi they never had to take seriously. Renzi made a nice pledge to the capital campaign. Much more than we could really afford—the widow's mite, you know? But that means nothing to them. Five thousand is nothing to them. Five million is something."

"Is that what she was giving? Five million?"

"That's what I heard."

"Now that she's dead, will the school get the money?" asked Page, leaning forward to stop a wayward soccer ball.

"I don't know," said Augusta.

Chapter 19

The municipal offices of Middle Essex were not overly impressive, considering that the town was the richest suburb in the state. They were housed in low, one-story brick buildings loosely based on Thomas Jefferson's design of the lawn at the University of Virginia. The current mayor of Middle Essex, Willis McHugh, had never liked them. He preferred his personal office downtown on the top floor of a building he owned, one of the city's tallest skyscrapers. He liked to look down on the world, and why not? It was, he knew, entirely appropriate that he should.

On Saturday morning, however, Willis McHugh was not able to look down on the world. He could merely look out and across the quadrangle outside the mayor's office. It was a boring patch of grass criss-crossed by brick sidewalks and dotted with cement benches donated in honor of civic leaders of the past. He sighed and considered for a moment what insignificant memorial he would now be expected to erect to the memory of the late Ethel Weinrich. This led him to contemplate the eventuality of his own death and the requisite monument that would be established in his name, and he wondered morosely where the meaning in it all was to be found. What was it all for? He stared out the window, his pudgy hands clasped behind his back, and scrolled forward through his mind looking for an answer. He was not, after all, a savage in the jungle, believing that the source of all power and goodness was in the sky. The answer was most certainly not in the sky. He knew better than that. The only prize was power, power on earth, and no one gave it to you. No, you had to take it. Goodness was a joke; loyalty was a sham; religion was an opiate for the weak. Believers were saps.

As he ruminated on the meaninglessness of life, an image of

Ethel Weinrich in his office, which had, of course, been *her* office for many years, formed in his mind. She had attempted to give him advice, and he had politely listened. *You're a clever boy, Willis, but cleverness is never enough. I was clever, and it brought me nothing but grief. Knowledge you'll find is not so much; it's endurance that matters. That and knowing that it is better to be envied than pitied.* Willis McHugh inhaled, suddenly filled with resolve and determined to find a fitting commemoration for the woman he now regretted having cheated and betrayed. She was dead, and he could afford to be generous. She had been his political mentor, after all. It was the least he could do.

He was still imagining his homage to Ethel Weinrich when the door to his office opened and George Crabtree walked in. McHugh turned and moved away from the window. The two men shook hands and the mayor offered a chair to Crabtree. "Sit down, George. Sit down," he said patting the other man's shoulder.

Crabtree sat down, sniffing. He drew a handkerchief from inside his jacket and blew his nose noisily. McHugh, he noted, had doused himself as usual with Bay Rum cologne making it practically impossible to breath. He slumped in the chair and fixed his elbows on the upholstered arms, tenting his fingers.

"So how is our man Buzz holding up?" asked the mayor, smiling as he sat behind his desk.

"Buzz seems to be doing just fine—at least he's operating on all cylinders currently intact. He's a bit distracted maybe, but who can blame him? It just shows that he cares after all." Crabtree smiled faintly, only one side of his mouth making the effort.

"Of course," agreed McHugh. "Of course, caring is good...Buzz is very attractive when he looks concerned. How's the board doing? I suppose they're being interviewed by the Major Case Squad?"

"Yes. Most of them today. They talked to Mason Holt yesterday."

"Your alibi, I hear," said McHugh winking.

"Yes," said Crabtree who wondered how the mayor was aware of that, but knew enough not to ask. He supposed he had spoken to Mason. "They talked to Buzz and me, as well as David Whittier and Renzi Stark."

"Renzi Stark? Jesus. I guess he'll get his 15 minutes in the spotlight out of this."

"It would appear that he was the last person to speak to Ethel before..."

"I can just hear him," interrupted the mayor, laughing. "'Sure, I was the last person to talk to Ethel. I offered to polish her shoes with my tongue, but she refused.'" He cackled at his own wit and George Crabtree feigned amusement by smiling weakly. "Too bad Stark doesn't have the balls to have actually done this...I always thought he was a grade A pain in the ass wannabee."

"Yes, he is that."

McHugh smiled and blew air through his nose. "So what's the word, George? What are people saying?"

"People are saying that Ethel threatened Stark and that, therefore, he has a motive."

"Good. Let 'em talk about Renzi—even if it *is* all bullshit...what else?"

"Not much else. Everyone seems to be genuinely shocked and confused by the whole thing. Nobody really takes the Renzi Stark scenario seriously. It's just something to talk about that's also mildly reassuring."

The mayor pursed his lips in a fish-like grimace, pondering the situation. "Something to talk about," he repeated. "I guess the talk is inevitable."

"Yes," agreed Crabtree. "It's certainly inevitable."

"What about Kruppenheim? I bet he's losing it."

"I know Buzz talked to him right away," drawled Crabtree. "He registered his deep concern, etcetera."

"Deep concern, my ass. I bet the first question out of his mouth was concerned with the amount of any planned gift the school is likely to expect."

The other man shrugged. "I wouldn't know about that, but I believe our esteemed board president wishes to speak at the memorial service."

"Jesus, no!" said McHugh pushing away from his desk and slapping his leg. "The son of a bitch has cohojnes, I'll say that. Poor old Ethel will be spinning in her grave."

"And why is that, Willis?" asked the dean, his eyes mere slits above his tented fingers.

"Why?" repeated the mayor. "Because she despised the son of a bitch, that's why. She thought he was 'a vulgar, nouveau-riche Semite'—not a member of the local Jewish aristocracy like, say, Lowell Lasky or Nigel Pomerantz whose families have been rich for over a hundred years."

"Oh, I see," said Crabtree, unconvinced, but yielding the

point out of boredom. He gazed as if through gauze at the other man whose mind continued to work in unfathomable ways behind his embarrassingly protuberant brow ridge.

"What about that Arno character?" asked the mayor. "Ethel's personal secretary. Who's keeping an eye on her?"

"The detectives have talked to her, but I don't..."

"Maybe you ought to get over there and check her out. Personal condolences, etc."

"Well, if you think I should."

"Yes, I do. She might know something." McHugh rubbed his face as if gauging whether he needed to shave. "Yeah. Bring her some flowers, lay it on thick. There's a big party tonight at Phil Phillips' house. Everybody will be there. I can determine the lay of the land. You go see Arno. Call me later tonight."

Chapter 20

"You've been awfully nice, Page, to listen to me," said Augusta Stark, edging forward in the green Adirondack chair. "And I thought maybe you could put in a word for Renzi with that detective?"

"What detective?"

"Well, aren't you dating the one…I thought I heard…"

"No, sorry," said Page, crossing her arms over her chest.

"Well, I should go," the other woman said quickly. "I've got to get Nick to the barber and pick up Janie before I go to my cooking class."

Page nodded, but made no move to get up. Augusta glanced around nervously. "If all goes well with this class, I may actually start that catering business I've talked about for so long."

Page nodded again but appeared not to be listening. "Do you know what I was thinking about earlier this morning?" she asked.

"Well, no," said Augusta, shaking her head.

"I was remembering that we read *Our Town* in the eighth grade and put it on for our parents and for the Middle School. I tried out for the part of Emily, but I didn't get it. I didn't emote enough. Instead I played Howie Newsome, the milk man."

"I was Emily," said Augusta.

Page laughed, then looked squarely into the other woman's eyes. "That play had a tremendous effect on me."

"Yes," agreed Augusta. "It's a good play."

"No," said Page leaning forward on her knees. "I mean it really *effected* me. Remember the third act—in the cemetery, after Emily has died?" Augusta nodded, remembering only vaguely, and Page continued. "Emily wants to go back and watch herself live one day, and she chooses her twelfth birthday, but she finds it unbearable to watch. Everyone is so blind, so oblivious. And Simon Stinson, the sinful choirmaster, says, *yes,* 'that's what it was to be alive. To move about in a cloud of ignorance; to go up and down trampling on the feelings of those about you. To spend and waste time as though you had a million years. To be always at the mercy of one self-centered passion, or another'...And Mrs. Gibbs says, no, there's more to it than that. But even in the eighth grade I recognized that what he said was true—that 'cloud of ignorance'—I lived in it! We all lived in it. We were all trampling on each other's feelings all the time. It was our way of life." Page sighed and looked down at her hands. "I just wanted to say, you and Renzi seem to have things straight, and your children are happy. Don't let those people trample on you. Turn away. They can't hurt you if you don't care what they think."

Augusta stared, her mouth rigid, not sure what to say. "Renzi could lose his *job,"* she finally stammered.

"And if that happened, what then? Would the world end? No. It would just mean you wouldn't have to go to those pretentious Whittier, Weinrich, and Goblenz Christmas parties."

"But, Page, you can say that...you've never..."

"I've never *what?*" said Page, her eyes wide. "I've never had to sell my big house and move? I've never had to take my children out of school and make them start over..."

"I'm sorry," mumbled Augusta.

"I have and I'm here to tell you it doesn't matter. Your friends who love you will still love you, and the ones you have because of where Renzi works, well, you never needed them. Renzi can find another job if he has to, and you and your family will be fine, you'll be better off."

Augusta stood up. "You have more faith than I do," she said waving to her son.

"You'll be all right, Gus," said Page, standing up. She reached for her classmate's arm, but stopped short of touching her. "The police will find the murderer. Don't get ahead of yourself."

Chapter 21

The cement walk leading to Stuart Bunting's brick bungalow was littered with brightly colored plastic toys. Pushing an overturned Cozy Coupe out of the way, the detectives proceeded to the door. They knocked, since the bell seemed to be out of order. Presently the door was opened by a disheveled toddler in a drooping diaper who stared silently at the two strangers.

"Is your daddy home?" asked Vesba. The child sucked on his binkie and did not reply.

"Hello?" called Merton. "Is anyone home?" He repeated the question.

The child stared.

Finally footsteps could be heard from the back of the house. "Orlando," scolded a thin, rabbity woman, whom they assumed was the baby's mother. "You know you're not supposed to answer the door!" Turning to the detectives, she smiled nervously and said, "May I help you? I'm afraid we don't need…"

"I'm Detective Roy Merton from the Major Case Squad ," interrupted Merton. "And this is my partner Detective Vesba. We're wondering if Stuart Bunting is at home?"

"Stuart? Stuart's my husband. What do you want with Stuart?" she asked, having turned several degrees paler than normal. She patted Orlando's head distractedly. The child stared.

"There's been a murder at the Rochester-Bingham School. We need to ask Mr. Bunting a few questions," said Merton. "Is he home?"

"A murder?" she gasped. The detectives nodded. "He's home. He's in the study. I'll show you."

Mrs. Bunting turned and, scooping up the child, led them down a dark hallway past the kitchen to a dingy room not much larger than a closet where a man sat hunched at a cluttered desk smoking and staring at a blank page in a manual typewriter. He looked up when his wife, after hesitating, tapped his shoulder and said, "Stuart, these detectives need to talk to you."

Bunting turned to the detectives, but said hello only after his wife had stepped back and receded into the hallway. A man in his late twenties with the look of one who has always spent too much time indoors, he seemed dazed as he listened to the detectives. He smiled when they told him about the murder at the school. "But what does that have to do with me?" he asked pleasantly. "I'm just a teacher. I don't get involved in board politics. People like Mrs. Weinrich have nothing to do with *teachers*."

"Even when that teacher is 'involved' with her granddaughter?" asked Leona, waving her hand through the smoke that continued to gather around her head. "Can we talk somewhere else?" she asked irritably.

Bunting stubbed out his cigarette and stood up. "Let's step outside," he said, his eyes having finally focused and his demeanor transformed at the word 'granddaughter'. The detectives followed him out onto a rickety wooden porch and into a small rectangular yard subdivided by a cement walk leading to a detached garage in need of paint. The teacher kicked aside a dump truck and a fire engine on his way to a wooden picnic table where they sat down. "I repeat," he said, leaning forward on his elbows. "What does this all have to do with me?"

"We saw some pictures that someone had sent Mrs. Weinrich. Someone who wanted to be paid $5 million," said Vesba.

"What pictures?" asked Bunting.

"Pictures of you and Julie Weinrich in a hammock. You weren't reading Shakespeare."

"Oh," he said expelling air noisily through his noise. "I still don't see..."

"Mrs. Weinrich was being blackmailed," continued Vesba in an indulgent tone. "Do you know anything about that?"

Bunting took a pack of cigarettes and a lighter out of his chest pocket and shook one out. "No, I don't," he said, inserting the cigarette between his lips and lighting it.

"Mrs. Weinrich's son, Carl Jr., was also being blackmailed," said Merton. "I suppose you don't know anything about that either."

"No, I don't," replied Bunting coldly.

"Had anyone contacted *you*?" asked Vesba.

"Do I look like someone who would be the target of blackmailers?" asked the teacher waving his hand in a slow 180-degree arc. "The splendor falls on castle walls..." He laughed ironically and sucked on his cigarette.

"The horns of Elfland faintly blowing," said Merton eyeing the other man critically. "Tell us, then, about you and Julie Weinrich."

Stuart Bunting sighed and swung his legs over the bench of the picnic table so that he was no longer facing the detectives on the other side. He leaned with his elbows backwards on the table. "Julie Weinrich is in my sophomore English class. She's not terribly interested in Tennyson, Detective, but she is eager to learn. She's no novice, I'll tell you that much."

"Where's the hammock?" asked Vesba.

"The hammock? Ah, yes...Willows whiten, aspens shiver...The hammock is in the yard of Julie's friend, Charity McCann, who just happens to live next door to Julie's grandmother. Very convenient for Julie. She tells her parents she's going to her grandmother's house, then she trysts with whomever at the McCann's. The parental units are seldom ever home. It's just Charity and her brother and a Dominican housekeeper who hardly speaks English. I'm quite sure no one has any idea of what's going on there..."

"You weren't her only partner?" asked Vesba.

"Oh, good lord, no, Detective. I was merely a passing fancy. You know, these girls grow up fast. It's not as if Julie Weinrich is so different from the other girls in her class. They're jaded by the time they're in Middle School. Sex is just another diversion...like drugs or a new car. I can't really see that this was worth $5 million to hush up."

The two detectives were pensive for a moment, both studying the teacher's narrow back. Then Vesba leaned forward. "What about you? Couldn't this impact your job? Or wouldn't they care at the Rochester-Bingham School?"

"But I wasn't being blackmailed," said Bunting.

"True," said Vesba persevering. "But mightn't Mrs. Weinrich have made trouble for *you*? She could have gotten you *fired*."

"Not without dragging her granddaughter's name into it, and if there's anything that self-styled old guard care about it's protecting their names."

"Even if it means allowing someone like you to keep teaching out there?" asked Merton.

"Even if," agreed Stuart Bunting, turning to look Roy in the eye. "And if they fired me, they'd have to get rid of others. Believe me, it's a whole lot easier to turn a blind eye. It's not as if anyone's been hurt..."

"I've heard enough," said Merton standing up. "Let's go, Leona."

"Sure," she said joining him. She stopped to stand by the teacher, her hand on her hip. "Just for the record, where were you Thursday night?"

Bunting closed his eyes, presumably to think. "I was attending a poetry reading with another teacher, Carla Levinson. She'll back me up if you want to check."

Vesba crossed her arms in front of her chest. "Does your wife know about your extra-curricular activities, Professor?"

The teacher looked shocked. "Of course not. Gillian doesn't have the imagination to understand, and she's got her hands full with Orlando and another one on the way. Why would I bother her with that information?"

Vesba remained planted where she stood and looked down at Bunting who seemed genuinely perplexed by her question. He passed his fingers over his long, limp blonde hair and gazed at the sky. "It's a beautiful day, Detective. You should try to enjoy it."

Chapter 22

Tal Hawthorne lay on his side on the couch in the den and regarded the legal pad before him. It was quite blank. Its large whiteness was intimidating. He was glad when his mother came in and distracted him.

"What are you doing, Tal?" she asked as she selected a CD and put it on. She sat down in the red leather chair and rested her feet on the ottoman. She was wearing gray rag socks and no shoes. Lyle Lovett began to sing and Page closed her eyes.

"I'm thinking," her son confided. He closed his eyes as well.

"About anything in particular?"

"Just this thing I have to write," he said holding up his blank pad.

"Thinking is good, Tal. Get your thoughts together and organized, then write..." She opened her eyes. "What's the paper supposed to be about?"

"Our Most Interesting Person."

"Huh," said Page. "Someone you know or someone you've just heard about?"

"Someone we know," said Tal rolling on his back, embracing the pad under his folded arms. "I have that part figured out. That's not my problem."

"No?"

"I haven't gotten permission to write yet. I think I should get permission first."

"From your most interesting person?"

"Yes."

"That would be polite, I suppose, but I think you could go ahead and write it, if you're having trouble making a connection."

"You do?" asked Tal doubtfully.

"Yes, I do."

73

Tal sighed and was thoughtful. When he spoke again it was without the careworn cadences of the troubled essayist. "Who was that lady, Mom? Why did she come over with her son?" He turned as he asked the second question and supported his head with his hand while leaning on his elbow.

"That was Augusta Stark. I went to school with her a long time ago."

"What were you talking about?" asked Tal. "She seemed worried."

"She was worried about something, but it'll be all right," said his mother who gazed across at her son with the semi-startled look of a parent who has once again underestimated the cognitive powers of its off-spring.

"Nick was nice, but Walter's a better soccer player," said Tal.

"You bet I am," said Walter strolling into the room. He swatted his brother's hair, then picked up his mother's feet and slid under them onto the ottoman. "Those North Woodward players are all losers."

"They won the game, Walter," Page reminded him.

"Only because the ref stunk and never called them for fouling. One of those dorks pushed me from behind and said, 'You suck'. He didn't get called or anything."

"The referee can't see—or hear—everything," said Page feebly. "You played well, honey. You did your best."

"Yeah," said Walter in a tone that suggested his mother was clueless. He rolled his eyes. "So who was the lady, Mom? Why'd you ask her over?"

"A woman was murdered at Rochester-Bingham. Roy Merton and Ms. Vesba are investigating."

"Murdered at your old school?" asked Tal leaning forward. "Cool."

"No. Not cool. Murder is never cool," said Page grabbing the arms of the chair as Walter stood up abruptly, dislodging her feet from his lap.

"You are such a stupid, little dork," Walter said to Tal on his way out of the room.

"I am not!" yelled Tal. "That guy was right: you suck!"

"Tal Hawthorne!" said his mother, compelled to reprimand her younger son since her older son was now out of range. "You know vulgar language like that is not allowed in this house!" She could hear her mother's voice even as the words escaped from her mouth and she stood up to cover the smile that escaped restraint.

"I'm sorry, Mommy," said Tal contritely.

"Just don't say that again."

"I won't."

"Now I've got to take a shower and get ready for Aunt Sally's party." She stepped toward the door.

Tal twisted around on the couch. "Are we coming too?"

"No, it isn't that kind of a party. Colleen is coming over."

"You're always going out and leaving us!" His mother did not respond. She was gone and Tal lay back on the couch. The distractions were over. He clutched his pad once again and tasted the eraser on the end of his pencil. Lyle Lovett continued to sing.

Chapter 23

No one seemed to be home at the McCann residence. There was no response, at least, to the doorbell or to Vesba's repeated and vigorous banging on the front door. "Let's walk around to the back," said Merton, swinging his head to indicate the direction he planned to take.

"I'm not wearing suitable shoes to go hiking all over," said Vesba, standing firm on the front walk.

"All right," agreed Merton, glancing at her unsuitable footwear. "I'll be back." He turned and jogged down the driveway which curved around behind the house. There was a Jeep Wrangler parked outside the four-car garage. He looked through the window. The keys dangled in the ignition. He sighed and scanned the yard which angled down from a large brick patio into a wooded leaf-covered area.

"Who are you?" said an unintentionally shrill voice.

Merton looked back at the house, but saw no one. "I'm Detective Roy Merton," he said to the house. "Who are you?"

A teenage boy in oversized khaki pants and a huge untucked polo shirt, which only accentuated his diminutive size, stepped forward from the shadows. "I'm Dylan McCann. I live here," he said in a surly manner that suggested that the detective was not only ignorant, but stupid as well. "What do you want? Do you have credentials or something...a badge?"

Merton reached inside his jacket and pulled out his shield. "Major Case Squad. I'm investigating the murder of Ethel Weinrich."

"She lives back there," said the teenager, pointing, adopting again the surly tone which suggested lack of brainpower on the detective's part. "Or she did. That's her house through the trees."

"I know," said Merton pleasantly. "I wonder if you could show me your hammock."

"Our hammock?" Dylan asked. He scratched his dyed-blond head. "I think the hammock is put away. It's past the season for...being outside."

"Where was it?" asked Merton. "Can you show me?"

"I guess," said Dylan slowly. "What does the hammock have to do with Mrs. Weinrich's murder?"

"Possibly nothing. Please indulge me."

Dylan shrugged. "Sure. Follow me." He jumped over the patio wall and headed down through the leaves. Roy followed him into the woods. When they reached what appeared to be the corner of the McCann's property, Dylan stopped. "My mother always raved about the English country garden at the Botanical Garden, so my father had one built for her. This part here is supposed to be like a little sanctuary, a place to meditate or something. The hammock goes here," he said pointing to a space between two trees.

"Does your mother spend much time here?" asked Merton.

"Are you kidding?" said Dylan, putting his hand on his stomach as he guffawed. He slapped his leg with his other hand and continued to mimic amusement. "That's a good one."

"It's rather secluded back here, isn't it?" asked Merton who, ignoring Dylan, was calculating the distance to the back of the Weinrich home which rose darkly behind the boy.

"Yeah, I guess," said Dylan checking his frivolity and jamming his hands in his pockets. "So what?"

"So nothing. Thanks for showing me." He scanned the area once more, smiled and began to walk back to the McCann's house. The boy followed closely on his heels.

Back at the house Dylan opened the door to the Jeep and hesitated. "We party back there sometimes in the summer, but we never bothered the old lady."

Roy gazed at the boy, who could not meet his eyes. "It isn't summer anymore. Don't you need a jacket or something?"

"Naw," said Dylan sniffling and wiping his nose with the back of his hand. "I'm fine, but..."

"Tell me, Dylan," said the detective, his eyes never leaving the boy's face. "Did you ever get the feeling someone was *watching* you back there?"

"Naw...*watching*? Who would be watching? There are hardly ever even any lights on in that house..."

"I see," said Merton. "Well, thank you for your help." He started to turn, but the boy stopped him.

"Hey, Detective," said Dylan eagerly. He paused, licking his lips. "Tell me, do you get to carry a gun?"

"Yes."

"A shoulder holster? That is so cool. Can I see it?"

"No."

The boy shrugged. "My dad has a whole case full of shotguns—for duck hunting. One of these days he's going to take me out and he's going to teach me how to shoot. A handgun would be cool though. Very cool."

Merton smiled blandly, forcing the hair that had stood up on the back of his neck to relax. Then he turned and loped back to the front of the house.

Chapter 24

Vesba surveyed the café from the booth that was dark and set off a bit from the rest of the tables. "This is romantic," she said. "Do you come here often?"

Merton finished wiping up the wet water rings and crumbs left by the previous customers with a napkin. He nodded at a couple of policeman who entered and were sitting down at the counter.

"Friends of yours?" asked Vesba.

"I introduced myself over at the station when I moved to my condo." He took a drink of his coffee and looked out the window at the traffic on the side street to hide his smile. "So what have we got?"

Vesba sighed dramatically. "An old lady who was the Queen of grudge-carrying."

Merton turned to face his partner. "With a grudge against practically everyone in town."

"She's angry with the Rochester-Bingham School because they aren't going along with her plan to build a park instead of an administration building…"

"But she has suddenly changed her will—years after cutting the school out—and left it $20 million."

"A lady who is being blackmailed…"

"In all probability by her own son…"

"Do you really think so?" asked Vesba leaning forward.

He nodded. "When did Arno say Mrs. Weinrich had received the pictures?"

"Wednesday. In the regular mail."

"But she'd been to see Whittier on Tuesday…"

"Yeah…And if the pictures had come earlier—say on Monday—that might explain why she might have been angry with Carl Jr. and decided to put the school back in the will…"

"Meaning there would be less for Carl Jr. ..."

"Making Carl Jr. mad enough to..."

"Kill his own mother?" Merton shook his head.

Vesba settled back in the booth. "And why would Arno lie for Carl Jr.?"

"If she was in the blackmail with him...She'd have known about the change..."

"Would she? Would Mrs. Weinrich have told her secretary? And who else? Who did she tell about the change in the will?"

"Why kill Mrs. Weinrich then? Why not wait until she changed it back?" said Merton. "I don't see a motive for Carl Jr. here."

"No...but why was he blackmailing his own mother?"

"The usual reason—for money," he said. "He's a small-timer. He thinks small. He said he didn't know about the change in the will and I tend to believe him."

"You really think..."

"I don't 'really think' anything yet," said Merton. "I'll tell you someone else Mrs. Weinrich was mad at though. Our old friend, the mayor—Willis McHugh. In her notebooks she devoted a lot of space to McHugh."

"The asshole probably has a special chapter in notebooks all over town."

The corners of Merton's mouth pulled back ever so slightly. "Carol Selby was on the level about Mrs. Weinrich hand-picking her own successor when she finally retired. She thought he'd be her mayoral clone, carrying on her pet projects and maintaining her official grudges. She imagined she could hold onto control that way...But she was wrong." Roy looked at the table. "Willis had other ideas."

"So she was nursing her grudge against him for how long?"

"Well, he's been in office for nearly eight years."

"And she's been sitting there waiting for the right moment to pounce."

"I wouldn't be surprised if this park at the school doesn't have something to do with her revenge on McHugh, but I haven't worked it all out..."

Vesba looked dreamily out the window and Merton sipped his coffee. The waitress came and topped their cups and inquired about their need for anything else. He shook his head and smiled. The waitress, who was not young, blushed and hurried away.

Vesba smiled and stretched and said, "Oh, by the way, I stopped in to see that chauffeur—Ryan—on my way home last night." She waited for her partner to raise an eyebrow, and when he did, she continued. "I asked him who it was who told him he could take the night off. He said it was Ms. Arno, as a matter of fact, not Mrs. Weinrich. Which makes sense considering what Renzi Stark said about her being such a lady and all and never making plans like that herself."

Merton nodded. "Sylvia must have had something on her mind when she did that."

"And when she lied to us about it," said Vesba. "I can't quite picture Sylvia whipping up any cherry tarts though, can you?"

Merton sighed. "No, not really. Perhaps she has a friend."

Vesba's eyes lit up. "Do you think she's a lesbian? Maybe we've got some weird sorority here of nympho-lesbo-killer-secretaries who…"

"Stop, Leona."

"All right," she said, looking disappointed. "But I think we need to talk to Ms. Arno again, don't you?"

"By all means," he said and slid out of the booth. He held a hand out to Leona who struggled to follow. He hesitated at the door when he realized that Leona had stayed behind to pay the check.

"Shall we call ahead?" asked Merton when she caught up to him. "Or should we surprise her?"

"Oh, let's surprise her—definitely," answered Vesba as she stumbled across the gravel parking lot in her high heels. "I want to see if she wears that old spinster get-up every day or just for the benefit of certain other people some of the time."

Chapter 25

A maid in a black dress and white starched apron answered the door and invited the detectives in. She explained that it was Ms. Arno's day off and that, as far as she knew, the secretary was in her quarters at the back of the house. She was reluctant to take them there, but when pressed, she agreed to do so.

Sylvia Arno's rooms were located on the second floor over the attached four-car garage. There were two entrances, an interior and exterior. The maid led them through the house to the door marked with an engraved card in a brass holder. The card read SYLVIA FRANCIS ARNO. After speaking to the maid through the door, Sylvia Arno eventually opened it and greeted the detectives, blocking the entrance with her body.

"May we come in for just a minute?" asked Vesba. She did so in a manner so brisk and cheerful that her partner stepped to the side to get a better view.

"Why don't we go downstairs to the drawing room where it's so much more pleasant," said Sylvia.

"Oh, but I see you have a lovely fire in your fireplace. How nice. Let's talk here," said Vesba pushing past the other woman into the tiny room as she spoke, so that Sylvia Arno, who was taken aback by the call, had no time to make up her mind. "Thank you so much," said Vesba.

Sylvia Arno pressed against the open door as Merton followed his partner inside. "Thank you," he said as he passed her.

"Well, we'll be all crowded in here..." said Sylvia casting about the room nervously. "I don't know where we'll sit."

"We'll be fine," said Vesba exuding geniality as she chose a place on the blue toile-print loveseat. "Roy, you sit over there in that chair. Ms. Arno can sit next to me." She patted the loveseat, and reluctantly Sylvia joined her. Merton stood at the mantel and studied a collection of Netsuke carvings.

"Isn't this nice?" said Vesba. "I bet you have a bedroom and a..."

"A bath, yes," said Sylvia. "Two rooms and a bath. It suits me just fine."

"I suppose you have cooking privileges?"

"Yes, of course," said Sylvia. "The kitchen is just downstairs."

"How convenient," said Leona. She scanned the room again. "And I bet your other room is decorated all in blue as well."

"Yes."

"Blue must be your favorite color."

"Yes. It was Mrs. Weinrich's as well. We decorated these rooms together. She let me choose everything."

"It's really lovely," said Leona as she crossed her legs and stared at Sylvia who sat nervously on the edge of the loveseat with her hands folded on her knees. Today, Vesba noted, she wore her hair down in a becoming style that made her look years younger. She wore a blue knit dress, which, though plain, did not look like something a nun would wear.

"So," said Vesba. "Your initials are SFA—like Saks Fifth Avenue."

"Yes," said Sylvia lowering her eyes.

Vesba sighed and glanced at her partner who still stood by the mantel and was now studying the framed print hanging there. He caught her look, however, and stepped to the chair and sat down. He took out his notebook and pen and leaned back in his chair, which was upholstered in a bright blue and white striped fabric that would have looked less incongruous in a nursery. "We have a few questions we'd like to ask you, ma'am, if you don't mind."

Sylvia Arno glanced from the detective beside her to the other and back again. "I don't understand," she said concentrating on Vesba. "I answered your questions yesterday. I thought you were through with me."

"We have a few more," said Vesba. "Just a few more." She put her thumb and forefinger together for emphasis.

"Oh." Sylvia folded her hands in her lap and squared her shoulders. "Well, all right go ahead."

Merton cleared his throat. "Did you know, ma'am, that Mrs. Weinrich went to see David Whittier on Tuesday?"

"On Tuesday?"

"Yes," he said.

"I suppose so."

"You suppose so?" he repeated.

"Well, yes, on Tuesday I was probably aware that she was going to see her attorney, but I'd forgotten."

"I see," said Merton. "Did she talk to you about that visit? Did she tell you that she changed her will?"

Sylvia looked up at him and then down again at her hands. "Mrs. Weinrich changed her will all the time. I don't remember if she told me this time..."

"You don't remember?" asked Vesba leaning forward. "I don't suppose you remember if she told you that she'd decided, after all those long years, to include a bequest to the school?"

"No, I don't remember," said Sylvia glancing away.

Merton stood up and picked his way between the furniture over to the window. He pulled up the shade and gazed out the dormer window. "What a nice view," he said.

"Oh sure," snapped Sylvia. "It's a great view of the driveway and the garden shed and..."

"The McCann's backyard," he interrupted in turn. "Isn't that Mrs. McCann's meditation garden?"

Sylvia stood up slowly and turned toward the window. Vesba's line of vision was now at the other woman's waist and she noted that her hands were once again clenching and unclenching. "What?" asked Sylvia. "What did you say?"

"I said you have a great view of Mrs. McCann's meditation garden. That would be where the hammock hangs usually, am I right?" He pointed to a shady spot between two trees.

"How would I know?" snapped Sylvia. "Why would I care?"

"Oh, I don't know," said Merton crossing his arms and leveling his gaze on Sylvia. "I can picture you in here some night ready to go to bed with a good book and maybe a cup of hot milk and suddenly you hear something...someone giggling and laughing." He paused, listening, then turned to the window. "You come to look out the window and turn out the lights for a better view. Sure enough, it's those teenagers from next door. They're partying, drinking maybe..."

"You're crazy."

"Am I? I bet it went on all summer...I bet it was annoying...until you noticed that one of the girls wore her hair in long blonde braids and you recognized her...It was Julie Weinrich, wasn't it? Ethel's granddaughter engaging in all kinds of acrobatics in the hammock."

"You're disgusting. I never saw any such thing!"

He turned back to the window. "You could take a pretty good picture from here with a telephoto lens—even better if you climbed out on the roof..."

"This is absurd! As if I would do such a thing!" She stared at the detectives and they stared back at her. "Maybe I saw some partying going on, but I never *watched*...I'm no voyeur...I didn't..."

"Do you have a camera?" asked Merton as he stepped to the bedroom door and opened it.

"You can't go in there!" shouted Sylvia lurching around the loveseat to follow him. "You have no right to go in there!"

He scanned the blue bedroom. A white canopy bed with ruffled bed linens and a large glass-front case full of dolls dominated it. He felt a strange cold presence, which caused him to turn around, and as he turned Sylvia Arno grabbed his arm and yanked him backwards toward the door.

"This may not be my house," she hissed through clenched teeth. "But I do have some rights."

Merton allowed himself to be dragged back into the other room, and was pleased to see his partner, standing by the tall mahogany secretary which she had opened in their absence, revealing a Nikon 35mm camera, complete with a telephoto lens. "Lookee here what I found!" she said.

"So what?" asked Sylvia, her teeth still clenched. "Lots of people have cameras."

"Yes, that's true," he said calmly. "But it does cause one to pause and do some rudimentary calculations."

"What?" said Sylvia, staring.

"Simple math," said Vesba who had returned to the loveseat. "Let's add up the circumstantial evidence, shall we? An old lady is being blackmailed. Someone has sent some nasty pictures of her 15 year-old granddaughter—with a teacher in a hammock—a shocking scene clearly visible from your room. You took the pictures, didn't you, Ms. Arno? You had the means and you had the motive."

"Maybe you even have a dark room!" suggested Merton. "If we go down to the basement, will we find one?"

"Oh, you think you're so clever, don't you?" asked Sylvia in a tight voice. "But you aren't. You're stupid...stupid and clumsy and wrong about everything. You shouldn't be here. I want you to leave right now."

"Well," said Vesba digging her fists into the loveseat and pushing herself up and out of it. "I guess we've worn out our welcome, Roy."

"Welcome? You were never welcome! I may have to call my attorney about this invasion of my privacy."

"And who would your attorney be?" asked Vesba tilting her head and smiling pleasantly. "Carl Jr. perhaps?"

"Please leave!" said Sylvia, pointing dramatically.

The detectives headed for the door through which they had entered, but Sylvia directed them to another door which led to the stairs and to the garage. "Go that way!" she pointed.

They obliged without comment and walked around the house, following the driveway. Merton looked up at the imposing brick structure as he climbed into Leona's car. "I guess they'll sell it now."

"It's probably worth an easy million or so, don't you think?" asked Leona.

"I guess. I wonder where dear Ms. Arno will go."

"Maybe she'll find herself in a nice furnished cell provided by the state. She can fix it up nice and cozy-like all in blue."

"It's funny how her little apartment was decorated the same way all these big fancy houses are with the artwork chosen because it matches the couch."

"Whether it's Elvis on black velvet or Picasso, it should match, shouldn't it? Isn't that what everyone does?"

"Maybe everyone does," he said. Then he braced himself as she took off down the driveway, barely pausing as she pulled out into the lane.

"I suppose you have a chair and a bookshelf, a candle maybe, and nothing else in your condo?" she asked.

"I have a damn good mattress," said Merton smiling.

Leona's laughter was cut off sharply as she swerved to avoid a car coming around a blind corner. "Asshole!" she screamed. "Jesus, that was close."

"Black Saab," said Merton, twisting back in his seat.

"Damn foreign cars," said Vesba. "I hate assholes in freaking foreign cars."

Chapter 26

"So what are you wearing tonight to Sally's?" asked Mason Holt as she walked into Ellen Chevalier's garage-sized closet. She scanned one wall of dresses, then turned to her friend impatiently.

Ellen looked up from a stack of mail through which she flipped distractedly. "What?" she asked.

"What are you wearing tonight?" Mason repeated. "To Sally's party."

"Oh, something I picked up last month when I was in New York. It's on the end there, in the bag."

Mason pulled the plastic bag up far enough to reveal a tiny fuzzy top over a gray satin skirt. "Oooo," she cooed. "Delicious. Anyone in particular you're hoping to impress?"

"No, stupid," said Ellen. "I haven't been lucky enough to break up any marriages lately."

"Are you implying I have?" said Mason icily.

"I'm not implying anything," shot back Ellen. She began to laugh and Mason joined her, grabbing Ellen's face in one hand.
"I hate you, you awful bitch." Mason let go of her friend's face with a final shake.

"Is George going with you tonight?" asked Ellen sweetly as she plopped onto a loveseat covered in red and yellow striped silk velvet which perfectly matched the red valencay silk fabric covering the walls.

"No. His wife just left town after all. We thought we'd wait a little before coming right out in the open," said Mason kneeling delicately next to Ellen, then flopping beside her. "He has his position at the school to think about."

"Oh, bullshit! He's got the missionary position to think about and that's all."

"What do you know about George and the missionary position?"

"Oh, nothing, please!" said Ellen in mock horror. She put her hand on Mason's arm. "Listen. If you're leaving George home to warm up the sack, why don't we go to the party together?"

"Oh, that won't work, Ellen. You know you'll want to stay longer than I will. I'm just going for Sally. Then I'll rush home to be with my George."

Ellen sighed and removed her hand. "Oh, Jesus, you sound just like you did back in high school."

"You're terrible, you know," said Mason sullenly. "You've just forgotten what it's like to be in love."

"I am married, don't forget."

"Oh, please. Lex hasn't been home in years! He's having too much fun down in Key West..."

"Cut it out!" warned Ellen throwing up one hand. "You know I adore Lex. He's been good to me and I won't have you saying bad things about him."

Mason eyed her friend and changed the subject. "I hear Phil is spending a quarter of a million dollars on this party for Sally."

"At least. He's planted a whole grove of baby Christmas trees—250—in the front yard so he could have them strung with little white Christmas lights." Ellen shrugged. "Then fairyland will be dug up next week and re-sodded."

"I drove by the other day. You'd think they were building a space shuttle or something...All the activity. It must be wonderful," mused Mason. "I mean, to have a spouse so adoring, and after being married all these years."

Ellen smirked. "If you say so," she said. Then, suddenly brightening, she added, "Hey, Mason, do you think Sally's little sister will be there?"

"Oh, I don't know...what's her name? Peggy? Patty?"

"*Page*," said Ellen impatiently. "Page Browning Hawthorne."

"Oh, her! She used to be married to Chester. I forgot for a minute."

"You forgot nothing. You know who I mean. She had the fling with the cop. I was just thinking it's too bad she won't be bringing him. He had those big gray eyes to die for..."

"Oh, him. I talked to him yesterday. He's not so much. What was all the fuss for? I'll never understand some people."

"What was all the fuss for?" mimicked Ellen.

Mason laughed. "Since when do you notice anyone's eyes anyway?"

"He's gorgeous," said Ellen. "But I guess you're so blinded by the glare bouncing off old George Crabtree's horn-rimmed glasses that you didn't notice."

Mason laughed again. "All right. I noticed...But he's really not my type. I like them a teensy bit more cerebral, don't you?"

Ellen nodded. "Oh, definitely. It's the size of their *brains* that's most important."

"That and a good sense of humor," said Mason with a straight face.

"And don't forget honesty."

"So important."

"And sensitivity."

"How could I forget? Smart, funny, honest, and sensitive—the perfect man. It's the size of his *heart* that matters to me," said Mason wheezing. She wiped the tears from her eyes with a needlepoint pillow.

"Well," said Ellen relaxing. "It's a shame he won't be there tonight to spice things up."

"Maybe," said Mason leaning back. "I just don't understand how you can take someone like that seriously though...how someone like Sally's sister could ever actually get serious? I don't get it. You have to have something in common to build a relationship. What do you talk about if you don't know the same people? If you don't have a shared past, or at the very least, a shared similar past? I'd die of boredom having to explain who everyone was, you know?"

"Well, it didn't work, did it?" Ellen glanced at her watch. "Oh, look, honey, I've got to start getting ready. You'll have to shoo. Go home now and leave me to my toilette."

Ellen jumped up and Mason followed more slowly. "You'll be the belle of the ball in that dress, Ellie," Mason drawled as she leaned in to kiss the air by Ellen's ear and grasped her friend's shoulders, squeezing. "I'll see you later, doll."

Chapter 27

Page finished brushing her hair just as she noticed the reflection of a dark blur go by in the bathroom mirror. She put on a quick swipe of lipstick and walked into her bedroom where Walter lay stretched across the double bed.

"What's up?" she said, smoothing the front of her dress.

"Nothing," said Walter.

"Well, then, tell me, how do I look?"

"Beautiful."

"You didn't even glance my way."

"You always look beautiful, Mom. I didn't need to look."

Page sat down on the edge of the bed and twisted around to lean on her elbow. "Is something bothering you? Something to do maybe with this murder investigation?"

"Maybe," said her son, still staring at the ceiling. "Maybe…"

"I wish you'd tell me."

"It's the same people involved in this case, isn't it? Like the one at Holy Comforter?"

"Sort of. Mrs. Weinrich went to Holy Comforter, but…"

"Did you know her?"

Page nodded, but since Walter was still staring at the ceiling, he didn't see.

"The blood of a murderer runs in these veins," he said holding up his wrists. "Does that mean that when I grow up I'll kill someone?"

Page sat up. "As far as I know they've never isolated a murder gene."

"Yeah, but you don't *know*."

She took a deep breath and held her hands in her lap to keep the one from pointing as she spoke. "Walter, you're a totally different person than your father… "

Walter flopped his arms down, resting his wrists once again on the bed above his head. "An honorable murderer, if you will; For naught I did in hate, but all in honor."

"I didn't know Shakespeare was in the fifth grade curriculum at Tucker Elementary."

"Ah, Mom, I looked 'murderer' up in *Bartlett's*!"

Page sighed. "What's really bothering you, Walter?"

"What if *this* murderer tries to hurt you?" Walter rolled over on his side away from his mother.

"Walter," Page said reaching for her son. "Whoever killed Mrs. Weinrich has no connection with me."

"Then why were you talking to that lady here today? What did she tell you?"

"Mrs. Stark was worried about her husband. He's a suspect and she…"

"You know *him*! You *have* a connection!"

"Walter, turn around. Look at me." Leaning again on her elbow, she pulled gently on his arm and rolled him over on his back so that he had to look up at her. She hooked a finger under his chin. "Look at me, Walter!" Grudgingly he opened his eyes and she continued. "Renzi Stark did not kill Mrs. Weinrich. I have nothing to worry about and neither do you."

Walter nodded and Page sat up, smoothing her dress. She stood up then and walked over to her dressing table. "Now leave me alone so I can finish getting ready. There's more to this job than you think."

Walter sat up. "Mom?" He waited for her to turn around again. "Tal's been brushing his teeth again after school."

"Oh," said Page, her shoulders sagging, as their eyes met. "I'll have to talk to him."

"I love you, Mom," he said before hurtling out of the room.

"I love you too," said Page to the empty room.

Chapter 28

"What's the mystery? You got plans or not? asked Vesba, eyeing her partner from across the desk.

He looked up from the stack of paper on his own desk and considered her question. "Yes, I do, but I'd like to go over our notes from today's interviews if you don't mind," he said.

"Fine. I don't mind a bit, but I've got to eat. I haven't had so much as a pickle since noon and I'm starving." Vesba got to her feet, signaling decisive action. "I'm going home; I'm out of here." He saluted her as she grabbed her purse and started for the door. Before she reached it, however, the door opened. The mayor, Willis McHugh, walked in. He was dressed in black tie, obviously on his way to another destination. He was not smiling. Vesba stopped abruptly and turned to glance at Merton.

"Working late, Detectives?" said the mayor.

"I was just leaving," she said.

"Good," said the mayor, cutting her off. "Why don't you run along. Your partner can fill me in." He smiled, then, at Vesba, and she wished he hadn't. His smiles were scarier than anything else his face could attempt to mimic.

She looked once again at Merton. He nodded, and she left. The mayor perched on the nearest desk and picked up a souvenir Rams football and tossed it in the air. He caught it, and pleased with himself, turned his attention to the other man. "I'm impressed," he said.

"Why's that?" said Merton, knowing a reply was expected.

McHugh looked around the room. He shrugged. "Well, here you are, working late. You're partner took off."

"She has a life."

"And you don't?" The mayor waited, but this time Merton

did not respond. McHugh continued. "You always take the back seat, don't you? Your partner talks to the press. You stand in the background. I hear you even let her drive. But somehow it's you people remember. Why is that, Roy?"

Roy shrugged. "Anyone in particular?"

"As a matter of fact, yes. I've had a call from Carol Selby. She was upset with both of you, but you especially."

Merton leaned back in his desk chair, crossed his arms and waited for the other man to continue.

"She said you were rude," said the mayor scowling.

"I hardly said a word to her."

Slowly the scowl dissolved into a grin. "Exactly. You let your fat partner take the lead. Carol likes men."

"She doesn't like me."

"Of course not, but she expects an appreciative up and down." He demonstrated, his eyes drifting up the detective's body and back down. Then he laughed. "Carol likes to be looked at, but not the way you looked at her."

"And how did I look at her?"

"Like you were trying to read her mind."

"Did she say that?"

"No, but I know." He shrugged. "And I know she's a self-important old crow. The thing is—and I know you understand this—Carol Selby is an important old crow, and a lot more important than you. You can't afford to antagonize important people like Carol. Not this time around."

Merton continued to stare. Then he leaned forward suddenly. "What exactly is the purpose of your visit today, sir?"

Willis McHugh, startled by the detective's move, stood up. Then the detective stood up. The mayor regretted it instantly as he was forced to look up into Merton's face. He looked down at the football in his hand and appeared to contemplate it. "This could be a big case for you, Roy. You might get a second chance at that promotion, but you're going to have to walk carefully. You ruffled some feathers the last time you came to Middle Essex for a visit." The mayor set the football down and redirected his flat brown eyes at a point beyond Merton's shoulder.

"Did I?" said Merton.

"You know you did. That business with Page Hawthorne was a big mistake. You overstepped and you got burned for your trouble. You do your job now and no more and everything should be all right."

Merton turned away. "You won't mind me asking you a question then?"

"Sure," said the mayor, relaxing, confident that he had hit his mark. "Shoot."

The detective turned back around and crossed his arms. "Where were you, sir, on the night of October 7 around 8:30 p.m.?"

The mayor stared, his mouth slightly ajar, for a moment or two. Then his eyebrows came together and wrinkles appeared on his face as it collapsed on itself. "What?" he asked.

"Where were you on Thursday night around 8:30 p.m.?" Merton repeated the words slowly as if the mayor did not speak English very well.

"I was in my car," said McHugh, speaking slowly also. "Driving home from a very long, very boring vestry meeting at Holy Comforter where I am now senior warden."

"You went straight home?"

"What are you suggesting?"

"Was there anyone at home who could verify..."

"No, as a matter of fact, my wife is in the Bahamas...the kids are with her."

"Oh, I see...too bad."

"Too bad? What do you mean, 'Too bad'?" The mayor's color had darkened and his mouth was a scar running parallel with his eyebrows.

The detective continued to ignore the other man's questions. He crossed his arms. "Mrs. Weinrich was the mayor of Middle Essex before you, wasn't she? She had high hopes for her successor, didn't she? She hand-picked you, but things didn't quite work out the way she had planned. You went your own way, hired your own people. She didn't like that..."

"And if she didn't, so what?" hissed McHugh.

"Her tough luck, right? Sure, except that Mrs. Weinrich was a true believer in the spiritual benefits of revenge."

"You think she could have touched me?"

"She thought so."

McHugh continued to stare, but his eyes slowly fell back into their sockets and the deep crevasses which transected the planes of his face, although not erased, eased somewhat. "She was a crazy old woman with delusions," he said.

"Uh huh," grunted Merton. "Well, sir, whether or not she

would have been able to bring you down is a moot point. She was going to try—maybe you knew that. Maybe that scared you just a little bit."

"Scared me? You have a hell of a lot of nerve saying that to me. That is total bullshit, and you know it."

"I don't know any such thing," said Merton. He uncrossed his arms and took a step toward McHugh who stepped forward too.

"Ethel Weinrich had nothing on me. She was my mother's cousin, for god's sake. Around here that means something."

"I'm sure that's why Mrs. Weinrich thought she could trust you." Merton smiled.

The mayor stared back, as if trying to remember something. "I've got somewhere to go," he said. As he turned he met Vesba blocking the door.

"I forgot my umbrella," she said shrugging.

The mayor looked at her without recognition. "Goodnight," he said and pushed passed her. The door slammed.

"You always seem to bring out the worst in him," said Vesba. "Why is that?"

"It's a mystery," said Merton.

Chapter 29

He pushed the doorbell, his heart beating like a teenager. He cursed himself and set his jaw.

The door opened, revealing one of the girls from across the street. She recognized him. "I didn't know you were the one taking Mrs. Hawthorne out tonight," she said.

One of his eyebrows rebelled. "I'm not." He stepped passed her into the front hall. "I came to see Tal."

"Tal?" she said, following him.

He strode into the kitchen, plunged his hands into his pockets and found change to rattle. He breathed in a combination of orange cleaner and baked bread.

"Billy?" called a familiar voice from another room. A door opened and suddenly she was there, wearing a black dress he recognized. It was an old dress that had belonged to her mother. Page had shown him a picture of her mother wearing the dress. She had bought the dress in Paris in 1961 on her honeymoon. She wore a hat as well and her arm was raised to hold down the hat with a gloved hand. The wind was blowing in Paris as Page's mother stood on some bridge and smiled for her new husband who must have been busy taking the picture.

She looked straight at him. "Zip me up?" she asked.

He stepped obligingly behind her. She smelled, as always, like soap and shampoo. He took hold of the zipper and eased it up her back.

"There's a little hook at the top too," she said.

He parted her hair at the nape of her neck and found the hook and the loop of thread and fastened them. He remembered this dress. He had unzipped it on another occasion, down to her tailbone, the longest zipper in couture history.

"I thought you were Billy Custer," she said without a hint of the anxiety he suddenly felt. Her fingers worked perfectly well, nimbly placing diamond studs on her exquisite ears.

"No," he said needlessly. "I'm not Billy."

"Why are you here?" she said. "What's up?"

He considered her question. "Tal left a rather cryptic message on my machine."

"Oh, I see," she said, as if what he said explained everything. She walked passed him to the door to the basement stairs, opened it, and called for her son. "He's coming," she said as thunderous footsteps verified her statement.

Then a small boy exploded through the door and launched himself at the detective's legs. "Roy!" he exclaimed. Merton leaned to embrace him as Page turned and walked out of the room. A door closed.

"Tal," he said, horrified by the tears that sprang to his eyes. "What's up, buddy?" He put the boy down and directed him to the den, a hand on his shoulder.

"I didn't think you'd come over," said Tal, dropping onto the ottoman as Merton sank into the red leather chair.

"I didn't quite understand your message. I thought I'd better talk to you in person."

Tal shrugged. "I have this paper to write about our most important person. I just wanted to get your permission to write about you."

"Oh," said Merton. "Did you ask your mother? What did she say?"

Tal nodded. "She said she didn't care who I wrote about, but I didn't need permission or anything. It was just a school paper and all." He shrugged again.

"But what are you going to say? Why are you writing about me?"

"You saved Mom's life!" he said. "And you were so nice to her when her shoulder was getting better and after that. She was so happy." He smiled at Merton, and he managed to smile back. Tal put a hand on Merton's knee. "I understand why you didn't marry her though."

He narrowed his eyes. "Tal, I don't think…"

"No," said Tal looking down. "My dad told us, Walter and me, a long time ago, back when we moved to our new house…that no one would ever marry Mommy because of us. No one would want us. They might want her, but not us. He said for the first time in his life he was glad we were there because of that, so we could ruin things for Mommy. He said we had ruined things for him, now it was her turn." He turned back to Merton and smiled.

Merton returned the boy's smile again, although this time it took every ounce of energy he had to do it, and reached over to touch Tal's shoulder. Tal stood up and Merton pulled him close. It had always been his policy not to be openly negative concerning Chester Hawthorne, but at times that verged on the impossible. "You know, Tal," he said finally. "Your father said a lot of strange things, things I don't agree with, but that is possibly the most..." He paused. "Well, it's just plain not true. I guess he felt bad and he wanted you to feel bad. Some people are like that." Out in the hall the doorbell rang and people started moving, distracting him for a moment. He looked down at Tal. "Someone told my son Peter when he was just a little boy that he had ruined my life just by being born. But being born wasn't his fault. Kids don't ask to be born. They shouldn't be blamed for what happens as a result."

"Who said that to Peter?" said Tal, pulling away from under Merton's arm to look him in the eye.

"My mother said it. She was upset. She had high hopes for me—thought I'd go to college and...Well, when I had to get married, that dream went away. But she had no right to say any such thing to a little boy."

"Was your mother mean?"

"No. Not really. Just very disappointed. The thing is, I did go to college later and things worked out, just in a different way. People get impatient."

"Mommy says that God has a plan for us all," said Tal.

"Yes, she does say that, doesn't she?" They smiled, man to man.

"Tal!" called Page from out in the hall. "Come say goodbye."

Tal bounded off his lap and headed out of the room. "Tal," called Merton. "Wait."

The boy stopped and lowered his shoulders as he faced the detective. "What?" he asked.

"Tal, I just wanted to say, maybe we should talk about this some more. I mean..."

"I'm fine," said Tal. "But if you want to talk, that's okay."

"Okay," said Merton. "I'll call you sometime." He put his hands on his knees and paused. Tal smiled and took off running.

Then Merton stood up and went out into the hall where Billy Custer was saying hello and goodbye to the boys, while Page gave last-minute instructions to Colleen. Custer was the old friend of Page's older brother who, as far as Merton could tell, was also her own best friend. He was handsome in his black dinner jacket. He must have come down from Chicago specifically for whatever event they were attending. Merton swallowed the negative feelings that were rising in his gut.

Walter noticed Merton first and sneered, turning away without saying anything. He cuffed his brother instead and said, "You're an idiot."

"Hey," countered Tal. "What did you do that for?"

"C'mon," said Billy, stepping between the boys and holding them at arms length. "Cool it."

Page glanced in Merton's direction. "Did you work things out with Tal?"

"Yes, I think so," he said.

"Hello, Roy," said Billy extending his hand and smiling. "Good to see you."

"Yeah. *Great* to see you," said Walter.

Roy shook the other man's hand and blinked at Walter. Then he crossed the length of the hallway to the door. "I'll get out of your way. Goodbye, Tal. Good luck on your paper." He turned and moved quickly out into the chill October air. It felt balmy compared to the atmosphere in the little house. He moved down the brick walk to his truck without looking back. When he reached the driveway, he heard something that caught him up and he turned around. It was Page clicking toward him in high heels.

She stopped at the top stair by the driveway and looked down at him. She was out of breath. He waited. She said, "Roy, I'm sorry. Don't just leave." He crossed his arms. "I have to go to this stupid 40th birthday party of my sister's. A command performance, you know. Billy's in town for the party and so we're going together. There'll be 200 people there." Merton looked away at the street. "Why don't you come?" she said. "No one would even notice. We could find some quiet corner and talk."

He still didn't say anything or look at her. He looked at a car that drove down the street. "You have plans, I guess. Do you have plans?" she asked.

He nodded. "I have plans."

"Of course you do," she said, looking disappointed. "I'm

sorry."

"Maybe I could drop by later," he said, surprising himself. "What's the address?"

"44 Upper Middle Essex Drive, off Middle Essex Rd. You remember."

"I remember," he said turning to look at her. "You shouldn't have run out here like that. You've lost all your curl." He pointed to his own hair as if that explained.

She smiled. "Who was I trying to kid?" she said shrugging. He felt disinclined to comment further so he stared at her until she looked away into the street. "I'll see you later then, Roy. Remember: 44 Upper Middle Essex." She glanced back once more, then she turned and ran back up the brick walk to the door and disappeared.

He stared after her. What were you thinking? You don't belong here he thought. The house itself seemed to judge him. The very ivy that covered its brick walls sneered at him. He turned and found his truck.

He drove away and headed down the road that led out of Rockville. He wondered what his plans were. He had lied twice. Once to Leona and now to Page. Well, not exactly to Leona. He had planned to go talk to Tal and he had done that. He hadn't expected Page to be going out, all dressed up and sparkling, while he hadn't shaved since his attempt in Leona's car the day before. What *had* he expected? He rubbed his chin absent-mindedly. Now he had a few hours to waste before he could make an appearance at Sally's enormous showpiece of a house. He felt mildly hungry, so he turned east toward the Trainwreck.

Chapter 30

She shoved the plate at him across the bar. He mumbled a thank you and pulled the plate over. He piled the lettuce and tomato on the burger and the bun on top and picked it up and took a bite. She was still looking at him, her arms crossed, her head lowered, as if she had never seen anyone eat a hamburger before. He smiled while chewing. "Good," he said, after taking a swallow of beer to wash it down.

"You eat too many burgers," she said. "You come in here 3 or 4 times a week and order a burger with lettuce and tomato and fries and a Corona. You need to eat better, a man your age."

He raised an eyebrow, but continued to eat without commenting.

"You need vegetables," she said.

"What are the lettuce and tomato?"

"They don't count. And neither does ketchup." She stepped forward and leaned on her elbows on the bar, resting her chin in her hands. "I could cook you something good for a change. Some steamed vegetables, maybe some grilled fish. You'd like that."

"Would I?" he asked.

"You would," she said looking up from under heavy eyelashes.

"How old are you, Tricia?" he asked.

"Old enough to cook. Look, I get off at 10. You could take me home and I could cook you something. You'd like my home cooking."

He poured some ketchup on his plate and started eating fries. He looked at her large blue eyes circled in black liner, her lashes thickly coated with mascara. Her lips were pouty and lacquered with pink gloss. Her teeth were not straight. "I bet I would, Tricia," he said smiling. "But I have somewhere to go later."

"Sure you do," she said, standing up. She picked up a bar rag and wiped the wet circles under his beer.

"I do," he said.

She made a disparaging sound with her tongue. "You never go anywhere, except here to eat a burger and drink two beers." She threw the rag down and placed her hands on her hips. "You ready for your second?"

"I sure am." He pushed the plate and unused cutlery forward.

She put them under the bar, then reached into the cooler for a Corona. She expertly popped the bottle cap and slid the beer across the bar. "You let me know if you change your mind about the cooking."

Chapter 31

The house was ablaze with lights, and as he came close he could feel the reverberations of an electric bass. He had been to the house only once before, at Christmas, which seemed like a hundred years ago. It had been similarly over-decorated then, and once again he was struck by the ludicrous and artificial quality of the forced gaiety. He sighed and looked skyward at the moon. The universe was still indifferent.

He smiled when the valet parking boys snickered as he handed them the keys to his truck. He smiled again at the expressionless butler who opened the door. When Sally appeared he smiled as he leaned to kiss the air by her ear. Her perfume was heavy and narcotic. Page's older sister, Merton noted, was not as beautiful as Page, but she was strikingly good-looking, handsome in a glossy magazine way. She was small like Page and also very thin. Her hair was dark brown with chemically-enhanced red highlights, and her eyes, her best feature, were large and brown and piercing. They studied him critically.

"Well, look who's here? Detective Tall, Dark and Dreary. And don't you look fabulous," she said insincerely. She put her hands on her hips and stood back. "Funny. I don't remember your name on the guest list."

He smiled indulgently. "Page asked me come," he said.

"Oh did she really?"

"Yes." He hoped his smile reflected warmth and not true feeling.

"Billy Custer's here," she said. "Why in the world would she ask you?"

He shrugged. "She did and I'm here," he said less warmly. He stared her down from a height advantage of nearly twelve inches. It wasn't easy.

"I'd turn right around and leave now if I were you."

"Where is she?"

Sally narrowed her eyes and waved her hand vaguely. "Around here somewhere. The last time I saw her she was tete a tete with Billy." She rolled her eyes in the direction of the long curving staircase. "They could be anywhere."

"She's on the dance floor," said Phil, Sally's enormous husband who had suddenly appeared behind her, an amazing feat for such a large, lumbering man. He circled her waist with his huge hands and picked her up like a puppet. "Don't you be mean to this boy, even if it is your birthday, Babykins."

"Put me down, Kong," she said patiently.

"Go on, go find Page," said Phil. "I'll keep Sally busy."

Merton forced a smile and turned as Phil embraced his wife, having set her down, and restrained her with noisy kisses from following. He did not look back.

In the Olympic sunken living room he moved through the crowd of overdressed, sequined bodies with canine focus until a firm feminine hand took hold of his arm and swung him around. Before his eyes could adjust the woman had grabbed his shoulders and pressed her mouth to his, prying it open with all the strength of her much-practiced tongue. He pulled away breathlessly to see a tall, tanned woman lick her lips, then throw back her head to laugh open-mouthed. Although he was not amused, he smiled cordially, even as his mind rifled through its file to place her. He had interviewed her when he was working on the Holy Comforter case. She had been one of the murder victim's many lovers. She had sought then, even on the day after the priest's death, to recruit him to fill the vacancy.

He looked on now, the memory registering, as Ellen Chevalier picked up her glass and a partially-chewed chicken wing. "So we meet again with champagne and a chicken, dear detective."

"Hello, Ms. Chevalier," he said, crossing his arms defensively. "And how are you?"

"I persevere despite the fact that I never did find a satisfactory replacement for the late great Reverend Costello. I don't suppose you'd be..."

"No," said Merton, jamming his hands into his pockets and scanning the crowd for a small golden head.

"I heard you were on the loose again." She leaned closer. He looked down. "I hear that you and your fat partner are investigating Ethel Weinrich's murder. Did I hear correctly?"

He nodded, diverted for the moment from scanning the room. "Did you know her?"

"Know her? Everyone knew Ethel!" She took a last sip of champagne and placed her empty glass on a tray passing by on the upheld palm of a waiter. She lifted a new glass from a tray passing by on her other side. She took a sip. "Ethel was a dreadful old woman with absolutely no sense of glamour. All that money and she was still wearing that le cirque hairdo and a 40-year old mink coat—I mean really! She was just a typical penny-pinching WASP dragon-lady who never knew how to enjoy her wealth." Ellen stopped talking for a moment and noticed the detective looking over her shoulder. She grasped his chin in her hand and wrenched his face back in line with her own fixed brown stare. "*Detective*," she said.

"Yes?" he said loosening her grip and dropping her hand which smelled of chicken.

"I'm going to tell you something, something important, because I like you so much and because I still have hopes for us..." The detective forced himself to look into her eyes. "Carl Jr. is in serious financial distress and has been for some time."

"With 150 million dollars?" he asked .

"The $150 million belongs—belonged—to his mother. She never gave him a dime...*while she was alive.*"

"Interesting," said Merton directing appreciative eyes at the woman.

"I'll say interesting. Maybe even worth another kiss?"

He smiled but shook his head. "Where's the dance floor?"

"Well, why didn't you say you wanted to dance?" she asked, clutching his sleeve.

He calmly removed her hand and said, "I didn't. I don't. Phil said Page was on the dance floor."

"Page? Well, what do you...I saw her here, but that was ages ago. She was with Billy, of course, looking very un peu d'amour, and then I saw them head into the library..."

"Thanks, Ms. Chevalier. Thanks for the information." He gave a quick two-finger salute. "See you around." She blinked and he disappeared into the crowd. She swallowed her champagne and turned to locate another passing waiter.

C.R. COMPTON

Chapter 32

"Oh look," drawled Tony Spitz nudging Willis McHugh in the ribs and spilling his own drink in the process. "Isn't that our old pal Detective Merton over there? Talking to Ellen Chevalier?"

McHugh glanced in the direction indicated by his friend, his interest peaked but fleeting. Then, as Ellen grabbed the detective's face and raised her own to within an inch of his, he focused his eyes and concentrated. "Yes, I suppose it is," he said.

"Where's his fat partner?" asked Spitz as he scanned the crowd.

"He isn't here on *business,*" said McHugh.

"Then why?" asked Spitz blandly. "I thought he and Page Hawthorne were no longer together...I mean, how unlikely was all that shit anyway? I still have goddam nightmares about that whole goddam episode, you know? I'm chased, sometimes by that fat detective, that partner...She catches me too and climbs on top of me and presses those big breasts against me and I start to suffocate and..."

"Jesus, Tony, you're shit-faced already!" said McHugh, still staring at Merton who was still talking to Ellen Chevalier who was still trying to press up against him. She looked pathetic, repulsive even, touching the likes of him. She was drunk, no doubt. He scanned the room looking for Page Hawthorne, but she did not appear to be anywhere around. He had last seen her an hour ago, laughing it up with that worthless nobody Billy Custer. He had talked to her briefly, meaningless banter which barely cloaked their true feelings for one another.

"I knew they'd never last," said Spitz. "Page and that detective, I mean. What would they *talk* about anyway?"

McHugh turned to the other man, aware suddenly that he

was still speaking to him. "What?"

"I said what do you think they talked about? Page and that detective."

McHugh sneered. "I doubt if they *talked* much at all."

Spitz blinked, his pale blue eyes watering, then snorted loudly. "Oh, good one, Will! Good one!"

"Shut up, you jackass," said McHugh, smiling slightly as the other man attempted to control himself, but his eyes narrowed as he stared at Roy Merton's back.

Chapter 33

"Isn't this a lovely party?" asked Mary Farrell Pinchot, gesturing with her champagne glass to the other women gathered in the Phillips' library. "I think it's probably the loveliest party I've been to in absolutely ages. Why it reminds me of a lovely party I attended at the governor's mansion the year I made my debut."

"Did you wear that dress?" asked Nancy Dillard under her breath for the benefit of Mason Holt who sat beside her. Both women snickered quietly while Mary Farrell pretended not to hear.

"Well, I just admire our hostess so much," continued Mary Farrell as she gazed at the gilt framed portrait of Sally Phillips over the mantel. "She's such a creative person. Imagine designing all these floral garlands and centerpieces, with all the different colors and ribbons and colors...seeing the big picture as it were."

"She hired Ben Solomon—that's as creative as Sally gets," said Mason. "She'd be the first to say so."

"Oh, I think she's just being humble, don't you? She's really a very talented person. Did you see the decorations she made for the Rochester-Bingham Trivia Night? They were adorable!" The other women who were seated together on the large tufted leather couch across from Mary Farrell nodded. "That took lots of imagination and creativity. I'd give anything to be as talented and creative as Sally."

"And as rich," said Nancy laughing. "Wouldn't we all! It'd even be worth being married to Phil. I didn't use to think so, but recently I've changed my mind."

"Oh no," broke in Mary Farrell. "I don't know how you can say that. Phil adores Sally—absolutely worships her. He'd do anything for her."

"That's what I mean," said Nancy. "There was a time when I really didn't care to be worshipped...but now I think I could deal with it."

"That depends on what you mean by 'worship,'" said Mason slyly. "In the marriage service in the old, old prayer book, the groom said, 'With my body I will worship you.' It was part of the vows. I like that idea actually. I like it a lot. It almost makes the love, honor and *obey* part palatable."

"But I don't think that's what Mary Farrell was talking about, were you, dear?" asked Nancy.

"No, not really," said Mary Farrell smoothing the taffeta skirt of her dress. "I wasn't referring to sex, if that's what you mean. I was talking about an *attitude,* the way Phil treats Sally, like she's a queen or something, a *goddess.*"

Mason laughed. "But I want to be a god-dess. You said I could be a god-dess." Mason laughed again, the careless cackling of the chronically unamused, and Nancy joined her.

Mary Farrell looked blank and pale and then suddenly tears appeared at the corners of her eyes. "No, no," she said. "You don't understand. It's the way Phil loves Sally. He's so sweet and gentle and *proud*! He never asks her to *do* anything, only to *be* who she is. He only has eyes for her—as if she's the most fantastic woman in the world and he can't believe how lucky he is to have her as his wife, like he's won the ultimate prize. I honestly believe he would *die* for her."

The two women stared. Finally Mason said, "I know what you mean, Mary Farrell. Really. And you're quite right." She knit her brow and pursed her lips to show how genuine her feelings were. Mary Farrell sniffed and lowered her eyes to her hands which she clasped tightly in her lap.

Nancy, not to be left out, and feeling uncomfortable with the serious turn taken in the conversation, said, "Speaking of love, guess who I saw a little while ago? That gorgeous detective, the one who killed Chester Hawthorne and then swept Page off her feet."

"Actually his partner killed Chester," said Mason.

Nancy murmured an acknowledgement, then took a deep breath. "Well, if I were Page, I'd be livid. I mean if I saw him here tonight, after he dumped her like that. The idea of coming to Sally's party…"

"I saw her," said Mason. "She didn't look livid to me."

"Yes, I saw her earlier, arm-in-arm with Billy Custer, looking very chummy," said Nancy winking.

Mason put her finger to her lips and hushed her friend.

"Look," she whispered, motioning to the twin leather couch facing them where Mary Farrell had either fallen asleep or passed out, her blonde head on a needlepoint pillow featuring a bulldog in a clown costume. "Now shhhh now, honeybelle. Our Georgia peach is making her debut in dreamland."

"Oh, finally!" hissed Nancy grabbing Mason's arm. "Now we can escape!"

"Yes, let's," said Mason picking up her full satin skirt and tiptoeing away. "We have done our charity work for the evening.!"

Chapter 34

Sally Phillips was a good dancer, graceful and confident. She wore a red dress and people noticed her and she smiled. "You look happy, Sal," said Willis McHugh as he caught her in his arms after swinging her out. "Absolutely dazzling."

"Not bad for a 40-year old dame, is that it?" she snapped. Her smile said she was pleased, however, and McHugh swung her around again in response.

When she was back in his arms, he said, "Tell me the truth—are you happy with the big guy, Sally? Or will you run away with me?"

"I'm happy, Willy, but you know me—I'm the practical one. Page is the romantic in my family."

His smile faded and his partner scanned the room as the band concluded the song. He did not release her. "Is that what Page is—romantic?"

"She believes in perfection."

He smirked. "I thought she knew better." Sally arched her back slightly to break his hold. McHugh did not yield, however, and he leaned in so that she could feel his breath on her face. "What's the detective doing here tonight, Sal? Did you invite him?"

"No, I didn't," said Sally standing very still. "I gather Page did."

"They're not getting back together?" he said, his teeth absurdly clenched.

"Of course not," said Sally, relaxing as she spotted another man approaching from the crowd. "What do you care anyway?"

"I don't care. I just don't like seeing him here. The bastard's not even wearing a tux."

Sally rolled her eyes and reached behind McHugh's shoulder.

The mayor's plastic smile vanished as Merton took Sally's hand. "How about a dance, Sally?" he asked softly as his eyes locked for a moment with those embedded like chocolate chips in the doughy face of the other man.

Sally sighed. "Why not?" she said, never glancing at McHugh as they danced away.

"You look relieved, Sally," he said a moment later. "Are you all right?"

"Of course," said Sally brightening. "Why wouldn't I be all right?"

"I don't know," he said. Sally looked away over his arm. "Did McHugh say something?"

She ignored his question. "Willis doesn't like you much, does he?"

"I suppose not—does it matter?"

"He's a powerful man, aside from being the mayor. You should be careful..."

"Careful?"

"Don't play dumb with me, Roy," said Sally as she raised her face to search his. "You know exactly what I mean. Watch your back." When he did not respond, she continued in a slightly less shrill tone. "A guy like Willis doesn't have the usual amusements. He gave up drinking years ago. He doesn't play golf and he's never been much interested in sex. And he's so rich, making money isn't as much fun for him as it once was. No. The mayor is only interested in power, and the only real amusement in life for him is controlling people...even ruining them when it's possible. Just look at what happened to Page's friend, the rector of Holy Comforter. He was run out of town on a rail. Page was terribly upset."

"But not you?"

"Let's just say, I know how to choose my battles."

"All right," said Merton smiling down at Sally. "Thanks for the advice, then, but there's nothing much here to ruin."

She fixed her eyes on his. "I hear you're investigating Ethel Weinrich's murder."

"That's right," he said.

"Ethel was one of my mother's oldest and dearest friends. I loved her—she was an old dear."

"I haven't heard that one yet."

She smiled. "Well, let's face it—as she got older, she became more and more difficult."

"Meaning what exactly?"

"She was very outspoken and opinionated. She never did or said anything that the powerful men in this town haven't done or said, but somehow when a woman acts that way…"

"Excuse me?" said Merton, trying to look shocked.

"I know," said Sally. "Terribly hypocritical—but Ethel trampled on a lot of people's feelings. She burned lots of people, although most of them may not even have known who it was who burned them." She chuckled. "Willis is her cousin, you know. They have a similar modus operandi."

"I've heard that." He swept the dance floor with his eyes.

Sally noted the distraction in the detective's gray gaze. "You're not a very good dancer, are you?" she said.

He looked down, unsmiling. "Just one of those advantages I didn't have as a kid."

She stopped. "I was just kidding," she said. "You're so serious." He did not respond so she took his arm and pulled him to the French door a few feet away. She opened it and stepped out onto the limestone patio, pulling him through. Then she released his arm and stepped to the balustrade where she paused, breathing in the night air. "I wasn't very nice to you when you arrived tonight," she said without turning around. He didn't say anything so she looked back over her shoulder. "I'm sorry. There's never any excuse for rudeness, is there? At least that's what my mother always said."

He still said nothing, so she turned around and crossed her arms. "Let's start over. I'm not so bad you know. You see all this and you make certain assumptions. But it could all be gone tomorrow and I wouldn't care. As long as I have Phil and the kids, I'll be just fine. I know what's important."

"Good for you," said Merton in the shadows.

She squinted trying to see him. "I had nothing to do with Page turning you down, Roy. She never asks my opinion on anything more important than needlepoint. Really. You shouldn't blame me or Phil."

"I don't."

"Good. We just want what's best for Page. We just want her to be happy."

He stepped out of the shadows and crossed the patio to stand next to her. He looked down into her upturned face, her unflinching eyes. "She needs you more than you think," he said. "Because this is all much harder than you think."

"I know," she said staring back at him. "Don't think I don't know how hard it is for Page. Everyone talking behind her back and everyone wondering about Chester and what she might have done to…believe me, I know. I've heard it all year, and I always defend her. In fact, no one dares talk in front of me anymore, they…"

"No, they wouldn't," he said quietly.

She turned away from him toward the forest of twinkling Christmas trees. "I would do anything for my sister. Anything. All she has to do is ask…"

"Maybe she doesn't want to ask."

She wiped something off her cheek. "Well, you didn't help her, not in the long run. You only made things worse, making your ridiculous demands and leaving. You didn't stay. I don't understand why you are here now. Roy, why are you here?"

"Let's just pretend I'm not," he said, turning to go.

"She's with Billy," she said turning back and placing a hand on his sleeve. "Why don't you leave her alone and let her get on with her life? She should marry Billy."

He stared at her. "Isn't Billy gay?"

She paused. She withdrew her hand and straightened her shoulders. "No, Billy is not gay," she said.

He shrugged. "Oh," he said. Then he turned and retreated into the house.

LEAVEN OF MALICE

Chapter 35

Merton had rapidly grown weary of fighting through the pressed bodies of Sally and Phil's 200 closest friends. Now he scanned again the sea of bobbing breasts and spandex-encased butts, teased hair and chemically-whitened teeth. None of these bodies belonged to Page.

He wondered vaguely if all these people were enjoying themselves. Did they ever relax, forget who they were and what was expected of them? Or were they constantly in competition with each other, forever figuring the expense of things? Who, they calculated, was wearing the most expensive dress, the most expensive jewels, the most expensive perfume, and did the answer indicate whose husband loved her the most, whose cheated the most? Who had had the most plastic surgery, the least? Whose business was in the most trouble? Whose practice was booming? Whose house was the biggest and furnished with the most expensive antiques? Whose ancestors were on those gilded walls anyway? Who the hell cared how much the flowers cost and that they had been flown in from somewhere exotic? *Who cared?* That was easy: everyone in this house, the lucky 200 who had been invited to Sally Phillips' 4oth birthday party. Everyone but him, he supposed, and maybe the girl he was looking for.

It was a mistake to pause, he realized too late as another hand clamped on his arm, forcing him to turn and interrupt his search for Page. This time it was a man who hailed him, a tall red-faced man who smiled broadly and seemed amused to see him. "Well, Detective," drawled Buzz Pinchot. "What a pleasant surprise...to find you sleuthing at Sally Phillips' party."

Merton's inanimate face did not reflect the other man's amusement, but rather, resignation. "I'm not here on business."

"Oh, my, then pleasure?" he said, lifting his eyebrows and his drink. "Did we talk about that yesterday?"

"No," said Merton. He studied the eager face that urged him to go on, but for some reason, perhaps because he wanted to find Page, not talk about her, he did not feel like cooperating, and he did not elucidate.

The headmaster smiled. "I do seem to remember now that George Crabtree may have made some mention of the fact that one of you detectives was acquainted with an alum, sort of in passing, a bit of trivia."

Merton nodded. "Trivia."

"Here's to trivia," said Pinchot as he raised his glass and emptied it. He shook his ice cubes, scrutinizing his glass for any remaining liquid. Finding none he looked at the silent detective. "Well, I hope you find what you're looking for, Mr. Merton. Maybe you'll be lucky tonight."

Merton nodded again and reached out to shake Pinchot's extended hand. "Maybe."

"In the meantime I'll endeavor to find my wife," said Buzz cheerfully.

Merton sighed and headed back for a second time through the huge industrial kitchen, made of stainless steel and marble and slate and used mostly, he suspected, by caterers such as the ones scurrying about now. He hurried to get out of their way, and bumped into Billy Custer backing away from an open refrigerator. Custer smiled, shook a lock of straight blond hair off his forehead, and held up a bottle of champagne. "Hail, Detective, well met," he said. "I suppose you're looking for Page."

"Yes," said Merton cautiously. "Do you know where she is?"

"She's in the upstairs study," said Custer, gesturing with the bottle. "Go up the back stairs, turn right and it's the first room on the left. She's waiting for you."

Merton nodded. "Thanks," he said.

"Oh, glad to be of service. Here, take this." He handed Merton the bottle of champagne.

Merton reached for it automatically. Then he turned and headed up the back stairs. He came out into a hallway and turned right. The first door on the left was ajar and a sliver of light shone on the carpeted floor. He knocked and pushed the door open. A small slender figure in black turned. "There you are," she said.

"It took me awhile to find you."

"Have you seen the forest of fairy lights?" she said turning back to the window. "Of course you have. How could you miss two hundred little Christmas trees planted and strung with lights, all to say 'happy birthday' to Sally?" She raised her glass of champagne and emptied it. "Of course, they'll all be dug up next week and the lawn re-sodded."

He took the glass out of her hand and set it on the table by the window. "A big gesture is about all Phil is up to these days," she said. "He does the best he can I guess."

He unwrapped the cork and opened the bottle without spilling, inwardly relieved. He filled her glass and handed it to her. She looked up into his face. She touched his elbow. "Let's sit down over here. I made a fire." She sat down in one of two matching salmon pink chairs, pulling her feet up.

He sat down in the chair next to hers and stretched his long legs out in front of the fire. He looked around the small room, at the framed pastel of three children over the mantel and an oil painting of a dog over glass-fronted bookshelves. He pointed to a black and white photograph of a much-younger Sally wearing a long, fancy dress, white gloves to her elbows and a plume on her head. "Was that when Sally was crowned queen of the universe?"

"Not queen," said Page. "She was a Special Maid actually."

"Were you a Special Maid?" he said, raising an eyebrow.

"No," she said sighing dramatically. "I was never a special anything."

"No comment," he said resting his head on the chair back.

She laughed, but he didn't. She took a deep breath. She looked sideways at him. "Comfortable?"

"Sure," he said, closing his eyes.

"I wouldn't want to keep you up."

"I'm all right," he said, folding his hands on his abdomen. "I suppose I'm just not used to the late hour."

"Early to bed and early to rise, make Roy healthy, wealthy and wise?"

He smiled faintly, without opening his eyes. "Yeah, something like that."

She cleared her throat and took a sip of wine. "I saw you on the news," she said. "The Ethel Weinrich case. You looked very handsome, very detached, letting Leona do all the talking. So, how's it going?"

"We've got a few leads," he said, rolling his head over to face her, once again surprised by her beauty. He swallowed his casual reply in a gulp of air.

"Is Renzi Stark a suspect?" she asked, unsuspecting.

"What?" he said, forcing himself to focus his attention.

"Today at Walter's soccer game Augusta Stark—Renzi's wife—came up to me. She wanted to talk," said Page. She cleared her throat again. "She told me Renzi was a suspect, that she was afraid the board was turning on him. I was sympathetic and listened, but I said I really didn't know anything. She was very upset and afraid of what could happen to Renzi."

"She so sure her husband didn't do it?"

"She's sure. She said Renzi never took Mrs. Weinrich's threats seriously. You know about the threats?"

Merton nodded. "How do you know her?" he asked.

"I went to Rochester Hall with Augusta. Renzi told her about you and Leona coming to see him."

"I don't understand. Why would she want to talk to you about the case?"

"She hoped I would put in a good word with you. I guess she didn't get the memo announcing our break up." Page leaned back in her chair and sipped her wine. Then she put it down. "Would you like some coffee?" she asked. "I could get some in the kitchen."

"Don't bother," said Merton.

Page stood up. "I'll be right back." She left the room with Merton's eyes on her back. When she was gone he closed his eyes again and listened to his heart foolishly pounding in his chest. Terra incognita. He tried to remember why he had thought it was a good idea to come here. He drained his glass of wine and put it on the floor by his chair. He ran his hands over his face, relieved that he had gone home after his dinner at the Trainwreck to shower and shave. He had debated the need, but remembering Leona's scathing words the morning before, had decided to clean up.

"Well," he said as she returned. He reached for the mug Page held out to him. He pulled himself up straight and took a sip. She settled back in her chair and waited. "So Ethel Weinrich, aged 73, was murdered in the cafeteria of the Rochester-Bingham School, between 8:30 and 9:30 p.m. on October 7," he said obligingly. "She was poisoned with a cherry tart."

"Sounds very Grimms' fairy tales."

"Leona thinks it sounds like a woman. Either way, we don't know who met her in the hall and offered her a tart."

"No finger prints I guess. No errant hair on the body or crumpled receipt from the Lake Forest Bakery?"

"No," said Merton. He looked at her sideways and sipped his coffee, then turned back to stare into the fire. "Mrs. Weinrich left the board meeting at approximately 8:15 p.m. She spoke to Renzi Stark who followed her out, and then, for some reason we do not know, she went downstairs to the Lunch Room. Libby Bancroft, Mason Holt and Cassie Cavanaugh went to the Ladies Room, and George Crabtree went to his office during the break. Mason Holt has verified that. Renzi Stark called his wife on his cell phone. That's been verified. Everyone else waited in the Blankenship Room and refilled their coffee cups and talked. At least that's what they say." He glanced at Page who was now staring at the fire. "Do you know Buzz Pinchot? What do you think of him?" he asked.

"No, I don't. I think Sally's gotten to be kind of friendly with his wife. According to her, Mrs. Pinchot is the type who keeps the home fires burning and the kids out of sight and never complains. Sally says Buzz tells her how to do everything—where to shop, where to volunteer, where and how to get her hair done...He's got her on a strict allowance and..."

"I didn't know men like that still existed," said Merton. "Especially in enlightened Middle Essex." He paused. "Leona thought he was charming when we talked to him the other day."

"But you didn't."

"No," he said taking a drink of his coffee. "I didn't." Merton glanced over at Page and back. "Anyway, there's a gap where we have no idea what was going on with Ethel Weinrich...It seems unlikely that someone—be it Renzi Stark, George Crabtree or Buzz Pinchot—could have convinced her to go down to the cafeteria, poisoned her, cleaned up, left her to die, and gotten back to the meeting, all during a fifteen-minute break."

"Unlikely, but not impossible," said Page. "So who else is there?"

"There's her son, Carl Jr., and her secretary, Sylvia Arno," he said. "And there's the added bonus of blackmail. It seems Carl Jr.'s fifteen-year old daughter was having sex with her English teacher..."

"What?" exclaimed Page, turning her head sharply.

"In the pictures it looked like they were on a hammock..."

"Pictures?" said Page.

"Two sets. The first set was sent to Carl Jr. who says he couldn't come up with the cash. Second set was sent to Grandma Ethel, asking for an upped ante of five million. The secretary says that she would have paid and that she had, in fact, done so before.

Ellen Chevalier says he was in financial trouble and had been for some time."

"When did you run into *her*?" asked Page with distaste.

"Tonight on my travels through Babylon," he said. "Looking for you."

She shivered visibly. "So do you believe him?"

"Yes, about the money, and that's easy enough to check," he said. "But I wonder...His reaction to those pictures, even considering he'd seen them before...didn't seem very...parental."

"So what are you saying?" asked Page. "Do you think he was blackmailing *himself*?"

"Yes," he said.

"Do you think he took the pictures himself?" said Page.

"He may have," he said. "Or he may have paid someone to take them. I don't think—if indeed it was Carl Jr.—he ever expected the police to become involved. He expected his mother to pay up, end of story." Roy stood up and walked to the window. "Carl Jr. seemed almost confused by the idea of the blackmailer coming back to him now that his mother can't pay. My money's on Carl Jr. blackmailing himself. There's some evidence to suggest that Sylvia Arno, his mother's secretary, may have helped him. If they were indeed involved in blackmailing Mrs. Weinrich, it casts doubt on their being involved in her *murder*."

"Unless his mother knew," said Page. "Would she have taken him out of her will or something like that?"

"No, she hadn't taken him out of the will. According to Carl Jr., she didn't get the pictures in the mail until Wednesday, the day after she went to see David Whittier, but that was a lie."

"He lied?" asked Page.

"Yes," he said. "The pictures were sent to Mrs. Weinrich on the previous Friday. We can't say for sure, but I bet she got them on Monday."

"But you say she didn't take Carl Jr. out of the will," said Page.

"No, but she put the Rochester-Bingham School back *in* the will. Personally I can't see him killing his mother because she changed the will. He was used to his mother doing that," said Merton. "It's more likely that someone *else* killed her to keep her from changing it back again."

"Which takes you back to the school. There could be several people with motives then—even Mr. Pinchot..."

"And then there are the notebooks," said Merton putting down his coffee mug. "The notebooks where Mrs. Weinrich made a detailed accounting of everyone who, over the last 45 or so years, had ever insulted her or hurt her feelings. She wrote down everything—and how she paid everyone back. I went through them all—over 3,000 entries—ranging from every small slight a woman endures to business setbacks and board room backbiting."

"Three thousand entries?" She appeared to let that statement sink in. "Remember Victor McLaglen's character in *The Quiet Man*? Maureen O'Hara's brother? He was always saying to his henchman, 'Write his name in the book.' He was a very controlling, unforgiving sort too."

He smiled and felt something inside him start to melt. He stopped smiling. "Sally said Mrs. Weinrich was a friend of your mother. How well did you know her?"

"Not that well. I knew her from church and my parents knew her socially, but..."

"Your mother's name was in the book," he said, cutting her off. "Lib Browning. 1966. She didn't agree to head up the Vassar volunteers for the Musée de Noel the year Mrs. Weinrich was chairman. A few years later, Lib didn't get picked to be Head of the Altar Guild."

"In 1966 my mother had Sally," said Page. "She was a little busy with a new baby...well, it doesn't matter now. The Altar Guild thing was important to her then though. Really important. It bothered her for years."

"I'm sorry," said Merton, clearing his throat. "That's just how Ethel got her kicks." He leaned forward and folded his hands. "There was a lot going on in her books around the time of the school merger. Mrs. Weinrich was dead-set against the two schools merging. She was counting on the new mayor, her hand-picked successor—Willis McHugh—to back her up."

"He didn't, though, did he?" said Page.

"No, not by a long shot. He sided early on with the pro-merger people and seemed to be quite instrumental in the whole thing. As the mayor his support was very advantageous. Mrs. Weinrich seemed to think he had something to do with acquiring the land between the two schools—the land that's at the center of the controversy now, the land she wanted to make into a park."

"What about Renzi Stark?" asked Page. "Did you find anything to suggest she was nursing a grudge against him?"

"I never saw Renzi Stark's name, but there were other board members listed...and, of course, George Crabtree."

"So you believe Renzi?"

"We can't cross Stark off our list just yet."

"Well," said Page gazing into the fire.

They were quiet for a while. Finally Merton leaned on his knees. "It's been nice talking to you about this," he said. "Like the proverbial old times."

Page, still staring into the fire, did not respond. Merton checked his watch. "But it's getting late. I should go."

"No, not yet," said Page, looking up. She uncurled her legs and stood up. She smoothed her dress. "How's Peter?" she said quickly. "Where did he decide to go to college?"

"He's at Washington U. We have dinner once a week."

"You must be so proud. He's done so well."

He stared at her. He was not thinking about his son. "Did I tell you how good you look?" he said.

"So do you," she said. She stepped over to him and stood in the 'v' formed by his legs.

He put his arms around her, pulling her close. He laid his head on the flat black front of her dress. His hands moved down to the top of her thighs and he pressed hard. Her hands went into his hair. The familiar feeling of their two bodies together caused them both to swallow their breath. A sigh escaped him, and her knees buckled. Then they both jerked their heads in the direction of the door when it suddenly opened.

It was Willis McHugh. "Oh, sorry," he said, recoiling at the scene that seemed to freeze for several seconds while no one breathed. Then McHugh coughed. "I was looking for the john."

"Across the hall," said Page.

McHugh paused, then shrunk backwards. The door closed. He was gone.

Merton struggled to gather his thoughts, then, not quite suppressing a growl, pushed her away. He stood up and stepped to the window. She stared at him, but said nothing. "Why don't you go find Billy," he whispered.

"Why?' she said moving to his side and resting her hand on his sleeve.

He looked down at her. Her eyes were large and amber and full of concern, but they held none of the pain that he felt, only questions. They wondered what he would do next. It was all up to him. "Why?" he said, apparently thinking. He bent down and kissed her. It was a hard kiss, a kiss that expressed nothing but confusion. When he stopped, he wiped his mouth with the back of his hand.

"Because where I come from, ma'am, a lady always goes home with the man who brought her."

She stepped back. She crossed her arms. "Was that supposed to hurt my feelings?"

He forced himself to meet her eyes, but he said nothing.

"Well, sorry, Wyatt Earp, you missed your mark."

He continued to stare, confusion clouding his focus. Finally he stepped to the door. "Tell Sally her party was nice and thank you for having me," he said.

"Fine," she said. "I'll do that. You go home now and suffer some more."

He turned and walked rapidly out into the hall and bumped a picture on the wall as he turned too sharply down the dark back stairs leading to the kitchen.

In the pantry he was caught up by a low, unhurried voice saying his name. Merton turned toward the voice. "I wouldn't be so fast to head back in there if I was you." Billy Custer was sitting on the stainless steel counter, leaning back against the tile wall by the sink. He held a champagne bottle in one hand, a glass in the other. The only light in the room was the one over the sink and it shone on his blonde hair, giving him an angelic aura and causing Merton to squint.

"Why not?" asked Merton.

"Because," said Custer. "Ellen Chevalier has been in here twice looking for you. Sneak out the back way is my advice."

Merton looked toward the hallway and escape. "What did she want?"

"*You*, Detective." He raised his bottle and laughed. Then he wiped the smile off his face with the hand that held the glass. "Which isn't really very funny," he said soberly. "Not really."

Merton walked to the refrigerator and opened it.

"That's the champagne refrigerator," said Custer. "The beer's in the basement. Mixers, I don't know where. Food's in the kitchen fridge."

Merton shut the refrigerator.

"She was very different in high school from the way she is now, you know," said Custer.

"Who?" said Merton.

"Ellen, of course. She was chubby and plain—nondescript. Not a whole lot of personality either...But she lived in that Bavarian castle off of Richenbaecher Road, complete with pool, tennis court, stables. It was always open and fully stocked with food and drink—including the Kornbelt family brew on tap. Her house was Party Central. Her parents were always out of town—leaving Herr Ohaus and his creepy wife, Edwina, in charge. Poor Ellen—the girls put up with her, because she indulged them, and the boys...well, you can guess."

"There are always girls like that. There always will be."

Custer nodded. "I remember Willis McHugh telling us all in the Senior Room one day how Ellen had made him a needlepoint belt for his birthday and how she'd sewed in her initials and his—you know, EK to WM. He refused to take the belt, saying he wouldn't wear it unless she took her initials out. And you know what? She did."

"Jesus," said Merton. "A sad story with a needlepoint belt tie-in. Where else but in Middle Essex?"

Custer ignored him. "She reinvented herself in college—dropped 50 pounds and became a real glamour girl. Then she married Lex Chevalier, the decorator. He lives in Key West most of the time now. Ellen gets lonely."

"I can handle her," said Merton.

"No doubt, Detective. But I thought you might not be in the mood." He glanced at the back stairs.

"Thanks for the warning," said Merton who stepped toward the hall and the back door.

"Page is struggling," said Custer, catching him up. "She's had a miserable year."

"So I've heard," said Merton, unable to keep a note of bitterness out of his voice.

"Things didn't go well?" he said under the unforgiving light.

Merton tried to stare at the other man, but he looked away and thrust his hands into his pockets, instinctively searching for his keys. They weren't there. He remembered that he would have to go find the valet parking guys and wait. "Where did you say the beer was?" he asked.

Custer threw himself off the counter, landing unsteadily on two feet. He placed the glass and the bottle carefully in the sink and brushed off the seat of his pants. "In the basement," he said, but the detective was already gone.

Chapter 36

The people leaving the Church of the Holy Comforter after the 8 o'clock service did not tarry, lingering in the garden to talk to their friends, because unlike other people on Sunday morning, they had places to go, people to see, golf games to play. They hurried to their cars, their minds full of the day ahead, having left behind in the dark church any and all spiritual concerns.

Willis McHugh looked at his wristwatch and shook down the sleeve of his dark gray suit. He scanned the street, noting the dark line of cars, his own black Lexus prominently parked a short distance away across the street. He had things to do, but he waited, knowing Mason Holt would be out soon. He could see her black Land Cruiser parked up the street. He blew air out his nostrils and folded his arms and cursed once again the fact that the church had no parking lot. With over 2000 members and three Sunday services that added up to a lot of cars. It was a circus every Sunday and the neighbors were not amused. Not that he cared what the lousy sons of bitches thought. They deserved to have the area rezoned so that the church could build a parking garage. A big cement eyesore that would send their real estate values plummeting. He could do it too. As the mayor he could swing it. Of course, the way things were going at the church, with membership sliding dramatically as everyone headed to the Presbyterian church down the road, the parking issue was becoming moot. They couldn't exactly finance a garage right now either.

McHugh twisted around as a bejeweled hand touched his shoulder lightly and a cool voice purred, "So, Willy, I hear you're looking for me."

He smiled. "Yes, Mason. Hi." He leaned over and brushed her cheek with his face and squeezed her arm. Then he gazed at her appreciatively for several seconds. "I do want to ask you a question."

"What?" she asked, looking over his shoulder, spotting her car. "That was a fabulous party last night, wasn't it? Phil really outdid himself this time. You'll have a hard time topping that when Mimi's 40th rolls around, won't you?"

"I'm afraid Mimi's 40th rolled by several years ago."

"Shame on you," said Mason, pushing his shoulder playfully.

The mayor smiled again. "Listen, Mason. I was wondering...Did you speak to George Crabtree or see him last night?"

Mason's face grew still. "As a matter of fact, no, and I...He said he was going to call and he didn't."

McHugh scowled. "He was supposed to call me and he didn't either."

"Do you think..." said Mason as she reached for his shoulder. "Should we..."

"No," he said swiping the air with his flattened hand. "No. I'm sure it's nothing. You go home and call *him*."

"I think I will," she said turning. "I'll just call him."

"That's a good idea. Call me if..."

"Call you if *what?*" The corners of her mouth turned down and her eyes were round with misgiving.

"Oh, nothing. Nothing. I'm sure he just fell asleep last night waiting for you. He's no doubt waiting for you now to get home from church."

"All right," said Mason. "If you think so, Willy."

"I know so," he said, squinting into the gray sky, trying to see into the future.

Chapter 37

The house where George Crabtree lived was a big one not far from the Rochester-Bingham School. Like most of the houses in the neighborhood it had been built in the Georgian style of dark red brick not long after WWII. "Our friend must have had some money of his own," mused Vesba as she pulled her car into the driveway which circled around to the back of the house and the two-car attached garage where several police cars and an ambulance were haphazardly parked already.

Merton scanned the scene, noting the white CSU van, the paramedics, and finally, sitting to the side of the garage on a brick wall and talking to a tall uniformed policewoman, Mason Holt. He gestured to his partner and they walked together over to the two women.

"Hello, Ms. Holt," said Merton nodding.

She dipped her head slightly and pulled the coat slung carelessly around her shoulders more tightly. She took a deep drag on the cigarette she held and looked away.

Merton turned to the policewoman and asked in a low voice, "Did she report the death?" The policewoman nodded. "We'll take it from here then," he said. "Thank you."

The policewoman walked away and Vesba sat down on the brick wall next to Mason Holt. "Can you tell us what happened, Ms. Holt?" she asked.

Mason searched Vesba's face with wide startled eyes. Mascara had run down her face and smeared on her cheeks. She looked years older than she had two days earlier. "George is dead," she whispered. "I found him."

"Yes, we know. We're so sorry."

"When did you find him?" asked Merton.

"About an hour ago or so...around 10:30. He was supposed to call me last night. He never did...I went to a party—Sally Phillips' birthday—in fact, you were there, Detective. I think I saw you." Merton nodded, ignoring his partner who shot him an inquiring look. "I came home around midnight. I waited up for awhile, but he never called. Finally I went to bed. After church this morning—the 8 o'clock service—I called him. Usually I wouldn't call him, but it wasn't like him not to call when he said he would. But he didn't answer the phone, and I was worried, so I just got in my car and came over here...and found him like this." She waved vaguely at the garage and at the black Saab inside. Very quietly she began to cry.

"What do you think happened, Ms. Holt?" asked Merton.

"Well, I know how it must look," began Mason, sniffling. "And I suppose, maybe, if George had been drinking, he might have passed out and..."

"Was Crabtree a drinker?" asked Leona.

"No, that's just it. George drank socially, of course, but I never saw him drunk. I don't think..."

"It was an accident?" said Vesba.

"No. I doubt it very much."

"What about suicide?" asked Merton sitting down on the other side of Mason Holt.

"Absolutely not," she answered, turning to face him. "George had a life, a good life. He was supposed to *call* me."

"He was separated from his wife and his children," he said. "Some people might find that situation pretty depressing."

"Yes, *some* people. But not my George. They had finally moved back east. The coast was almost clear for us."

"Almost clear?" asked Vesba.

"We were in love," said Mason, leaning forward on her knees. "He would never have killed himself. He had too much to live for."

"He didn't seem like the suicide type," said Vesba as an aside to her partner.

The other woman heard her and said, "He wasn't. You're right about that. He thought people who killed themselves were weak. He said the idea of suicide is really just like a great consolation..."

"Consolation?" repeated Vesba.

"By means of it one gets successfully through many a bad night," quoted Merton.

Vesba looked blank.

"You know, a person can always kill himself *tomorrow*," explained Merton. "At least that's what Nietzsche thought.

"Exactly," said Mason. "George agreed with Nietzsche."

Vesba rolled her eyes behind the other woman's back and motioned to her partner to leave them alone.

Merton stood up and excused himself. He headed over to the Medical Examiner whom he had recognized earlier.

"Hello, Roy," said the tall, bald man leaving the garage. He ran his hand over his hairless head reflexively and sighed. "I suppose you'd like to know how and how long ago?"

Merton crossed his arms. "Yes," he said. "How and how long ago?"

"Carbon monoxide poisoning about 12-14 hours ago."

"Suicide?"

"I don't think so. We'll test for alcohol level in the blood and rule out an accident, but I think...It looks to me like murder."

"How so?"

"The guy has a nasty bump on the back of his head."

"Fatal?"

"No—probably just enough to knock him out. Someone seatbelted him into his car and left him to die. I've never seen a suicide wearing a seatbelt." He tipped an imaginary hat. "We'll do more tests and get back to you."

"Thanks, Jerry," said Merton. He turned around to walk back to the wall but stopped when he saw Mason Holt sobbing on his partner's shoulder. He walked instead to Vesba's car and waited.

When Vesba finally joined him, having returned Mason Holt to the capable hands of the statuesque policewoman, she looked him up and down. "Don't you look nice this morning. What got into you?" she said.

He looked down at his chest as if to remind himself what he was wearing. He noted the Brooks Brothers suit and striped tie. He grumbled.

"Decided to get in the game?" she asked. "You look just like the corpse."

"Thanks," he said. "So you obviously believed her."

"Yes, I did. Didn't you?" said Vesba, leaning against her door with folded arms.

"I suppose."

"Oh, bullshit. Tell me what you really think."

"I was just a little surprised by her emotional reaction."

"I think she may have been too."

He nodded. "When we talked to her on Friday she was...Well, I wouldn't have guessed she was so emotionally involved with Crabtree."

Vesba regarded her partner with uncertainty. He seemed confused. She took a deep breath loudly through her nose. "I think she cared for him, but like a lot of these rich bitches we've become acquainted with, she took the situation largely for granted, like they take everything for granted. Then, when the situation changed—tragically—she wasn't prepared."

"I suppose so."

"Well, listen, she did tell me one thing. She said Crabtree wasn't wearing his horn rims when she found the body. She said he was practically blind without them. He couldn't have driven an inch without his glasses."

"They probably got knocked off when he was hit from behind."

"What?" she said taking a step forward to look at her partner. "What did Jerry say?"

"Jerry said he had a big bump on the back of his head."

"So it was murder?" Vesba sighed, stepping back and leaning again against the car. "You think someone shut him up?"

"It looks that way."

"So what did brother Crabtree know that would have gotten him killed?"

"And where have I seen that black Saab before?" he asked as he gazed into the garage.

Vesba followed his gaze into the garage. Both were thoughtful as they watched the CSU team work around and inside the car. Then suddenly Leona straightened up as a large black Lexus pulled around the corner. "Look who's here," she said. "An official visitor." Merton swore under his breath. "Do you think we could sneak away?" she said.

"Not a chance," he said as the mayor pulled himself out of his big black car. He saw them and started over in their direction. The detectives waited, arms folded.

"What gives?" said McHugh loudly. "Tell me George Crabtree isn't really dead."

"Carbon monoxide poisoning," said Vesba nodding toward the garage. "Last night."

"Have they determined if it was an accident or suicide?" asked the mayor.

"Not officially," said Vesba. "But it looks suspicious."

"Oh Jesus Christ," said the mayor spitting out the words. "What do you mean suspicious? Are you talking about another goddam murder?" He turned to Roy. "So while you were up the road at Sally Phillips' party, someone iced old George Crabtree right under your nose?"

The detectives said nothing. Merton gazed placidly at the mayor and Vesba raised an eyebrow at her partner. She popped her gum and smiled when McHugh shot her a disdainful look.

"So what are you doing about this, Detectives? Jesus, I talked to him myself just yesterday. He was..." The mayor stopped abruptly as both detectives straightened up and focused sharply on him.

"What?" he asked.

"You spoke to him?" asked Merton. "When yesterday? What time?"

For a moment the mayor's lips seemed frozen in a fishy expression of confusion. Finally they pushed forward and open and he breathed again. "What does my having spoken to him have to do with anything? I don't see a connection."

"It just might be helpful to know. We need to know what Crabtree was doing last night. You wouldn't happen to know?" asked Merton.

"I talked to him in the morning...in my office. Just a friendly chat," said McHugh changing his tone. "I have no idea what his plans were for the evening." He looked away, and catching sight of Mason Holt, began to move in her direction. He turned back for a moment. "Excuse me, Detectives, but I see an old friend in need of consolation." They watched as the mayor walked to the wall with outstretched arms. He embraced Mason Holt who was weeping again.

Chapter 38

The headmaster's house was large and brick and set on two and a half acres of park-like land adjacent to the southwest corner of the Rochester-Bingham School. Vesba whistled as she walked up the curving brick walk to the front door. "I suppose the house comes with the job? Nice work if you can get it," she said taking the gum out of her mouth and putting it in a wad of Kleenex.

"If you don't mind kissing ass for a living," said her partner who had hardly looked at the house. He stared at the welcome mat which featured a large silhouette of a Labrador retriever, and waited for someone to come and open the door.

Vesba regarded her reflection in the glass window panel to the right of the door and sucked in her stomach. She fluffed her hair. Satisfied, she turned back to the door as it opened and smiled at the tall headmaster. "Sorry to bother you on Sunday afternoon," she said stepping into the hallway. "But something's come up."

Buzz Pinchot stepped aside for the detectives. "What exactly has come up? I'm supposed to meet John Kruppenheim for a round of golf..."

"Well, Mr. Pinchot," said Vesba, cutting him off. "We're sorry to have to tell you that George Crabtree was found exfixiated this morning in his garage. He's dead."

"Suicide? George *killed* himself?" asked Pinchot as he stumbled to a spindly Windsor chair and collapsed into it. Several framed photographs on the table next to him fell over.

"Maybe," said Merton stepping over to the table and righting the photographs. "Maybe not."

"Maybe *not?*" asked Pinchot. "In this zipcode carbon monoxide poisoning always equals suicide. Just six months ago Doris Morgan killed herself after her husband cut up her credit cards!"

"Nevertheless, this time it may not be suicide," said Vesba. She thrust her hand toward him but resisted touching him. "Are you all right?"

The headmaster looked up at her, his blue eyes round and staring, the corners of his mouth pulled painfully back. "I just wasn't prepared for *this*."

"Is there somewhere we can talk?" asked Merton.

"My study," said Pinchot after a moment. With some effort he stood up, extending his arm to the back of the house, and led them to a room with large windows through which the school was visible in the distance. Several framed pictures of hunting dogs hung on the dark green walls. "Have a seat. Please," he said as he lowered himself, groaning, onto a plaid sofa.

Vesba sat down at the opposite end of the sofa. Merton remained standing but moved to the window and gazed at the yard where two golden retrievers lounged.

Pinchot wrung his hands. "First Ethel...now this...Do you think there's a connection? Do you think George..." He broke off, unwilling apparently to finish the sentence.

"Do you?" asked Merton, turning to face the other man.

"Well, I don't know. I was just thinking out loud. What do *you* think?" asked Pinchot.

"We don't know, Mr. Pinchot. A connection seems likely, but..."

"But *what*? What aren't you telling me? I have a right to know. Did he leave a note? A suicide note?"

"Whether or not his death was a suicide has not been established," said Vesba.

"No? But carbon monoxide poisoning...in the garage? Like I said, that's usually the case, isn't it? Suicide, I mean."

"Often, yes," said Vesba, calmly watching the increasingly distraught man. "But sometimes deaths like this are accidental. Murder in this fashion is not unheard of."

"Murder? Oh, good lord, no!" The headmaster plunged his face into his hands once again.

Vesba leaned toward the headmaster. "Was Mr. Crabtree depressed or despondent? Had anything happened lately that might have upset him?"

Pinchot raised his face to look at the detective. "Well, yes, actually...I suppose...His wife had taken their children and moved back east. He said it was just a temporary separation, that they'd be back, but I doubted that very much. Muriel hated the Midwest—she saw it as a vast cultural wasteland—she couldn't wait to leave."

"What about Mason Holt?" asked Merton. "Couldn't she have been the reason his wife left him?"

"Well, I can see how you might think that, but, no, that wasn't the reason. Mason was just filling a void. George was devastated really."

Merton took out his pad and pen from inside his jacket and jotted something down. Then he raised his eyes and stared at the headmaster who gazed intently at his own laced fingers. "Why do you think there might be a connection between the two deaths?" asked the detective. "Do you have reason to believe that George Crabtree was involved somehow in the murder of Ethel Weinrich?"

The headmaster did not look up. He swallowed audibly. "Well, it's just that George...It's just that he despised Ethel so. He hated her, absolutely hated her...and he'd been so upset by Muriel taking the children. It's possible that Ethel's latest campaign—to establish the park—was just too much. He must have snapped. And then he may have felt so guilty, so terrible..."

"Why did Crabtree hate Mrs. Weinrich?" interrupted Merton.

Slowly Pinchot raised his eyes. "He never liked her, but he...his feelings changed toward her after he visited her home once alone. He had to...he went there to pick something up. She was always thinking of reasons to have me or one of a dozen charitable foundation representatives drop by for some reason. Sometimes I'd send George to represent me. One time—last spring, I think—he came back absolutely livid. After that he couldn't look at Ethel without..."

"What exactly happened?" asked Merton.

"He never actually said," said Pinchot. "I assumed it had something to do with the secretary...and Ethel...with their relationship."

"Why did you 'assume'?" said Merton.

The headmaster smiled weakly. "I don't know. He used to refer to the secretary as 'Alice B.', as in Toklas, and, well, he could be pretty snide. At the last board meeting, it was something George said that sent her out of the room..."

"Why didn't you mention this before, Mr. Pinchot?"

A flicker of relief passed across the headmaster's face and he half-smiled. "Well, I…didn't want to say anything that might shed a negative light on George. He was…But now that he's dead and…"

"Can't defend himself?" said Merton. He turned back to the window. "Where were you last night, sir?"

"Well, *you* know, Detective. I was at Sally's party. I talked to you there. I talked to lots of people, probably a hundred or more!"

"It was a big party," agreed Merton looking over his shoulder at Pinchot. "A person could get lost in a party like that."

"Yes, I suppose so." The two men stared at each other.

"So when did you leave?" asked Merton.

"About 11:30 I think."

"And then what?"

"I had a drink with my wife at home and then we went to bed."

"Together?"

"Yes *together*. I never left the house again if that's what you're wondering."

"We're sorry to have to bother you like this," said Merton amiably. "We'll check with your wife and then go."

"I'm afraid my wife is not home. She's still at church—at St. John's on Beasley Road."

"We'll find her…Thank you for your time, Mr. Pinchot." He extended his hand to shake as his partner slowly rose from her place on the sofa. Her knees cracked loudly and she grimaced.

"Goodbye, Mr. Pinchot," she said.

The headmaster shook their hands and said goodbye. "Has this story—about George—been released to the press yet?" he asked when they were halfway to the door of the study.

"I don't know," said Roy, turning.

"I can see the headline: 'Another murder connected to the exclusive Rochester-Bingham School,'" said Pinchot. "How long I wonder until 'exclusive' becomes 'beleaguered'? How long?"

Chapter 39

"You didn't believe him, did you?" asked Vesba as she rifled through her handbag for a piece of gum.

"No," said Merton. "I didn't. Did you?"

She thought a moment as she situated herself in the driver's seat of her car. "I don't know," she said finally. "Do we have a good reason not to or are you just suspicious of all these guys?"

He expelled air through his nose and slumped on his side of the car. "It may not be official yet, but what Jerry said about the bump on the head..."

"And no glasses..."

"Yes—I think we can assume he was murdered. The question is why would Pinchot try so strenuously to make us think it was suicide? George Crabtree never struck me as the depressed type and that business about Mrs. Weinrich being a lesbian—that was bullshit."

"Why? We'd even thought of it before, the other day in the coffee shop."

"It occurred to you, Leona, not to me."

"You yourself thought there was something funny about those two—remember Arno's room? The canopy bed, the dolls?"

"Don't you think Crabtree himself would have told us if he'd really thought so? It would have delighted him to make that kind of accusation and he could have pointed the finger at Sylvia Arno in the bargain."

Vesba murmured her agreement. "Assuming it was a lie, why would he lie *now*?"

"Why would he suggest that George Crabtree was the murderer unless he wanted to deflect our attention away from someone else and away from the possibility that Crabtree himself was murdered?"

"Maybe he just saw an opportunity to end the investigation. You know, wrap it all up by pinning it on the dear departed dean."

"So much for justice."

"But the school could avoid 'beleaguered' status."

"I suppose that could motivate him to lie," said Merton. "But there would still be a murderer out there. How could he turn a blind eye to that? How could he not care if we found Mrs. Weinrich's murderer when it happened right there on his campus?"

"I don't know," she said. "Come to think of it though, Crabtree wasn't upset either when we talked to him. He must have known that a murder on campus might adversely affect the school, but he didn't seem the least bit troubled."

"Yes, but he wouldn't take the heat—his boss would."

"He could afford to sit back and watch?"

"And maybe when he was watching, he saw something he shouldn't have," said Merton, straightening up.

"Something that got him killed."

"Let's go find Mrs. Pinchot at St. John's."

Vesba placed a chubby hand on his arm. "Wait a minute," she said. "Not so fast. Three people now have mentioned an interesting little fact, a fact which I'm sure you hoped I wouldn't notice." She paused, but he said nothing. "You were at that party last night, weren't you?"

"Yes, I was."

"Why?" she asked as if she really were surprised by his admission. "Were you invited?"

"No," he said, turning away and staring out the window. "Not by Sally anyway. I went over late, after ten, to see Page."

Vesba gasped. "What for?"

"I'd gone over to see Tal earlier," he said impatiently. "And she asked me then…"

She grabbed his arm and pulled him around. "Look at me," she said. "Look me in the eye and tell me you…I thought you…"

His gray eyes were hard and steady and she could not look at him. He shook his arm free. "Tal called me at work. There was a message I didn't understand. I thought I'd better go see what he needed…"

"You actually went over to her house?"

"I did."

"And she asked you to come to her sister's party?" She

crossed her arms and stared through the windshield. "Did you sleep with her?"

He grunted. She looked sideways at him, her eyebrows raised expectantly.

"Have I ever asked you a question like that?" he said. She didn't answer, but stared. "No," he answered for her. "I haven't."

"Excuse me for caring about you," she said petulantly. "For not wanting you to be hurt again."

"Look," he said. "I'm not some kid. It was no big deal."

"Roy and Page talking like two adults. That must have been a pretty scene." Vesba glared at his profile. "So what, now, are you going to see her again?"

"I doubt it."

"Really?" she said. "No sparks?"

He sighed. "Her sister Sally wants her to marry her friend Billy Custer. She was with him."

"Oh," she said, as though she saw the whole picture finally, but it was modern art and she didn't understand it. "I thought he was gay."

He smiled. "I think Sally would like it if Page moved out of town, up to Chicago. Take her problems elsewhere."

"Typical rich person response. Send the problem away." He nodded, but still gazed out the window. "So," she persevered. "Do you think she'll actually marry this Billy guy?"

He shrugged. "I don't think getting married is in her plans..." His voice faded off.

"I'm sorry," she said. "I didn't mean to dredge up a lot of bad old feelings, but I just wish you'd been honest with me."

"I'll remind you that you didn't tell me about Jerry."

"Yeah," she said. "Well I was thinking about your feelings."

He closed his eyes and laughed. "My feelings."

She growled.

"It's not important," he said with a glance that said the conversation was over. "Let's go find Mrs. Pinchot."

"Fine," she said and she plunged her foot onto the gas pedal. The car screeched out of the headmaster's gravel driveway, but the driver, at last, was silent.

Chapter 40

The parking lot of St. John's Episcopal Church was practically empty, most members who attended the third service of the morning at 11:15 having left long ago. St. John's was a brick colonial-style church with immaculate green lawns shaded by strategically placed oak trees and transected by brick sidewalks. One large green Suburban was visible at the end of the lot, and one lone woman was ushering four children into it.

"Let's ask her," said Vesba pointing. "Maybe she can help us."

Merton did not wait for his partner who was powdering her nose, but jogged over to the petite blond woman who was struggling to put a toddler into a baby seat in the back seat. She was short and the truck was tall. "You've got your hands full there, don't you?" he said, smiling at her as he lifted the child easily into the seat and buckled her in. He cast his eyes about the car, counting four children: one boy and three girls. The girls all wore matching navy blue dresses with white collars piped in red and a bunch of fabric cherries at each throat. He looked down at the woman who stared back at him. The stare was vacant; the woman looked drugged.

"Thank you," she said. "That was very nice."

"Glad to help," said Merton. "These trucks are huge, aren't they?"

"Yes. My husband bought it for me. He says everyone's driving one."

He nodded. "We're looking for Mrs. Pinchot. Mary Farrell Pinchot. Could you..."

"Why, *I am* Mary Farrell Pinchot," said the woman, putting her hand on her chest to indicate herself.

Merton grasped her other hand and shook it. "I'm Detective

Roy Merton and this is my partner Detective Leona Vesba." He held his hand out toward Vesba who had just walked up to the SUV.

Mrs. Pinchot's smile disappeared and her pale face turned paler. "*Detectives*? Why do you want to talk to *me*?"

"Could we..." asked Merton nodding to the children who were unnaturally quiet and staring in their direction.

"Of course," said Mrs. Pinchot. "Children, I need to talk to...these people. I'll just be a minute. Now, Hampton, you'll be in charge."

"Yes, Mama," said the boy in the back row.

Merton took Mrs. Pinchot's elbow and guided her a few feet to the edge of a formal garden surrounded by a black wrought iron fence. Vesba followed. The three of them stood in a triangle facing inward, arms crossed over their chests.

"Ma'am, we just have a few questions. We won't keep you from your family long."

"Thank you, but I don't understand. Is this about Ethel Weinrich?" stammered Mrs. Pinchot.

"Actually, ma'am, there's been another death." He paused as Mrs. Pinchot gasped. "George Crabtree died last night. Carbon monoxide poisoning in his garage."

"George *killed* himself? I don't believe it!" whispered Mrs. Pinchot.

The detectives' eyes fluttered up and met, immediately separating. "We're not sure yet whether it *was* suicide, ma'am. What we need to know from you is where your husband was last night. We're checking around. It's just routine..."

"What? I don't understand. Didn't you ask him? We were at Sally Phillips' birthday party...You were there, Detective, weren't you? I think I saw you." She pointed to Merton accusingly.

"Yes. I was there," he said. "I spoke to Mr. Pinchot as a matter of fact. When did you leave the party?"

"Not until after 12:30 I think."

"Together?"

"Of course."

"Did you see much of your husband at the party?"

Mrs. Pinchot's face, like a mask, seemed unable to change expression. "No. I never see Buzz at parties. He says parties are work—so he has to work, not keep me company. I've learned to fend for myself. I talk to my girlfriends. I entertain myself."

"And last night?"

"Buzz came to find me around 12:30. I was in the library taking a little nap. I've been very tired lately—it's probably the stress of this murder investigation. That's what Buzz says anyway. We went home, and I checked on the children. When I came downstairs Buzz was on the phone." She put her hand to her cheek. "No wait. He wasn't on the phone. He was standing *by* the phone, making a drink. We had a nightcap and then I went up to bed around 1:30. He came up later."

"Are you sure?" asked Vesba stepping forward.

Mary Farrell stepped back. "I was asleep I guess…I slept in. He had already left for church when I got up. Buzz goes to the 8 o'clock service so he can have the rest of the day to play golf or whatever. I teach Sunday School at 11:15 so…" Her voice faded out and she glanced at the green truck. "I need to take my children home."

"Of course," said Merton. "Who was babysitting your children last night?"

"We have a live-in au pair, a girl from Switzerland. She was asleep when we got home."

"I see. You've been helpful and we appreciate your cooperation. I just have one more question." He paused and she nodded. "What kind of car does your husband drive?"

She touched her cheek again and thought for a moment. "Why Buzz drives a black Lexus. Lou Otto—from the Otto Automart—gave it to him."

"Thank you," said Vesba, but Mrs. Pinchot was already scurrying away to her truck.

The detectives faced each other. Vesba shook her head as the truck roared away. "So who the hell do you think the headmaster was talking to on the phone at that time of night? And why do you care about the car he drives?"

Merton squinted and blew air through the circle of his mouth. Vesba, losing patience as she rummaged in her purse for her keys, said, "Roy, what are you thinking?"

He placed his hands on his hips and turned to his partner. "Much of madness," he said. "And more of sin, and horror the soul of plot."

She waved his words away as if dispersing a cloud of smoke. "You would know," she said.

Chapter 41

"I heard about George Crabtree, darling," said Ellen Chevalier. "This new twist must complicate things for you."

"Uh huh," said Merton leaning back in his chair balancing on two of its legs. He mouthed the name of his caller to Vesba and she nodded.

"Well, ever since I heard about it from poor Mason, I've been sitting here mulling it all over in my brain, trying to make sense of what's happened and..." She paused and took a drink, rattling ice cubes. "Detective?"

"Yes?" he said.

"Well, I wondered, Detective, if perhaps you'd like to come over this evening and help me make sense of it all."

"I don't..." he began, dropping his chair down on all four legs.

"No, no, Detective, don't turn me down so fast. You'd be surprised how much I know. Remember what I told you Saturday night at Sally's party? That was just the tiny tip of the iceberg. I know a *lot* more, honey. Especially about Carl Jr. and his mother."

"Hold on a minute, will you?" he asked and then held the phone to his chest, covering the mouthpiece. "Are you leaving?" he asked his partner.

"Yeah. I'm dead," she answered. "Unless you need me for anything."

"No, Leona, go ahead home. You don't need to wait for me." He waved her away.

"You sure?" she asked, slinging her purse over her shoulder and gathering up her coat.

He nodded. "Go on home."

She paused briefly, engaging his wandering eyes momentarily

until he smiled. "Okay then. I'll see you tomorrow."

"Tomorrow," he agreed. Then he lowered his head as she turned and left the room. "Ms. Chevalier, couldn't we just continue our conversation on the phone?"

"No! Oh no. That wouldn't be any fun at all."

"This is a murder investigation. Generally they're not fun."

"Oh," said Ellen yawning. "Well...I just thought I might be able to help."

"We appreciate that," he said hesitating. "But my partner has gone home. Maybe we could stop by for a few minutes tomorrow morning."

"What's this 'we' business?" asked Ellen suddenly caustic.

"Leona Vesba and I, my partner and I."

"Oh, no, no, honey. That wouldn't do either. I don't want her. I couldn't think with *her* here. No. Just you. The two of us, putting our heads together, combining our resources in a mental alliance. I'd make it worth your while, honey," said Ellen, her tone once again ingratiating. "Don't you worry. You come over tonight and I'll give you what you need. I won't hold anything back."

"All right," said Merton, his eyes flickering to his partner's chair and back to his desk blotter. "What time?"

"Oh, sevenish, I think," said Ellen. "I'll be ready for you by then."

"I really can't stay long."

"Just long enough."

"All right. Seven."

"Goodbye, Detective," she said. She hung up the phone and turned, lifting her glass in salute. "I'm good, aren't I?"

"The best," said the man sitting at the end of the leather couch. "A real pro, baby."

Chapter 42

He remembered the house—stately, rectangular and stone, like half a dozen other new houses sprinkled through this neighborhood of boxy brick mansions. He parked his truck in the circular drive and got out. He scanned the lawn and the façade of the house, wondering if she had asked him to come after seven, when it was dark, so that her neighbors wouldn't notice the truck parked in front of her house. No, on the contrary, Ellen Chevalier would probably relish the idea of her neighbors putting two and two together and coming up with five.

He rang the doorbell, and she answered the door herself almost immediately. He smiled and she returned his smile and laughed pointlessly. "No butler?" he asked. "No maid?"

"No one tonight, Detective. I sent them all home." Her eyes tracked up his body and she made no attempt to hide it.

"Am I early?" he asked.

"Early? Why no. You're right on the button." Her eyes slid to his face. "Why do you ask?"

"Well, I thought maybe...I'd be happy to wait while you finish getting dressed."

"Oh, you're adorable!" she said, dismissing his suggestion as she patted his cheek. "Now follow me, honey." Then she turned on a slippered foot and glided across the wide front hallway, down another hallway, passed a huge, immaculate kitchen to a large square room decorated completely in beige. The carpet was beige, the sectional leather sofa was beige, the open drapes and blinds were beige. The large paintings on the walls all depicted beige landscapes. The fireplace was beige marble, but the fire snapping inside it offered warmth and color. Merton instinctively stepped in front of it and warmed his hands.

"Will you have a drink with me, darling?" asked Ellen

Chevalier as she stepped to the beige bar.

"No thanks," he answered, reaching inside his jacket for his notebook and pen. He looked around for a chair, but there was only the sectional sofa. He smiled at Ellen, who, having made herself a scotch on the rocks, leaped enthusiastically onto the sofa and settled noisily into the corner of it. Her silk robe fluttered and came to rest, revealing a tanned expanse of thigh. She did not rearrange it, but patted the leather, saying, "Sit, honey. Sit down next to me here."

He sat down on the edge of the section that curved away from her. "Now, ma'am," he said. "What's this you said you had to tell me that couldn't wait 'til tomorrow?"

"Oh," she said taking a large sip of amber liquid. "Business first. I see. Well, Detective, let's be civilized about this. Tell me something about yourself," she said eagerly. "Where do you come from, for instance? Are the rumors true?"

"What rumors?" he said without enthusiasm as he opened his notebook and searched for a blank page.

"Oh, you know. The rumors about your humble beginnings, growing up in the 60s version of a log cabin—a trailer park. Did you live in a double-wide with your family in Jefferson County?" She swung her roving eyes up and down his body until they settled on his placid, unperturbed face, urging him to reveal his secrets.

"No, ma'am. I grew up in a nice little town up north on the river."

"No trailer park? No tornadoes?" He shook his head. Ellen leaned back against the couch and narrowed her eyes at the detective. "I suppose you never sang in a country western band called the *Dixie Road Apples* either?"

"No."

"You were never a stunt double for the dark-haired boy on *The Dukes of Hazzard?*"

Merton chuckled. "No."

Ellen smiled exposing her perfect teeth. "I bet you had no idea you were such a popular topic of conversation."

He closed his eyes. He shook his head.

"People love to talk, and women love a mystery man!" She laughed shrilly and placed her hand lightly on her throat.

Although he continued to smile, his eyes were blank, the pupils pinpoints.

"Well, let me ask you then, Detective Merton, what is it you need to know most about the Weinrich family, because, as a matter of fact, I know quite a lot about the scrubby Dutchmen. They're from Southtown originally—did you know that? The Weinrichs and my family, the Kornbelts, came to this country about the same time—the 1850s or so—with all those imbecilic Germans! They thought Missouri looked like Bavaria. The Ozarks, the Alps—go figure! But there were lots of Germans already here, so they came. The Weinrichs and the Kornbelts, both families, did real well. They were butchers and bakers and probably candlestick makers. The Weinrichs, being Protestant, rose faster, making better marriages, leaving Southtown sooner. But we caught up eventually. Now we could buy the Weinrichs ten times over, but...what was it I was going to tell you? Do you remember?"

Merton leaned forward on his knees. "Last night you told me Carl Jr. is having financial difficulties. How do you know that?"

"Everybody knows that! It's nothing new..." Her hands flew to her face. "Oh, now you'll think I lured you here under false pretenses. But that's not true, darling. My pretenses are utterly reliable. Anyway, even though they knew, no one else told you, did they?" She leaned forward, balancing herself on her left hand. The top of her robe gaped open.

"No," he said. "No one mentioned that."

Ellen emptied her glass. She licked her lips and stared at him as he gazed at the notebook on his knee. "Do I make you uncomfortable, Detective?"

"How do you know so much about Carl Jr.?" he asked, ignoring her question and the relentless eyes of his hostess.

She sighed. "Carl Jr. was my lover fifteen years ago." She put her glass on the large stone table and crawled sideways on the sofa. "He was older than I—and so naturally I thought he could teach me a lot. Unfortunately, it was the other way around, and I taught him a lot."

"Doesn't he have a 15-year old daughter?"

"Yes. Julia. His wife was expecting at the time...I gather she kicked him out of the bedroom once she was pregnant. You'd be surprised how many women do that or maybe that's just something men say...but I digress." She slid closer.

"Did someone find out about you and Carl Jr. and blackmail him?"

"I have no idea if anyone knew about us. I expect so, but no one tried to blackmail me—and I would have been a likelier target than Carl Jr."

"Who else was Carl Jr. carrying on with?"

"No one at the *same time*...I was more than enough for Carl Jr. to handle. But *before* me, he'd had a brief fling with a paralegal at the firm. I believe Sylvia Arno was her name." She paused, waiting for a reaction.

"The same Sylvia Arno who became Mrs. Weinrich's secretary?" he asked.

"The same," said Ellen stretching her arm across the back of the sofa and brushing the detective's shoulder with her long-nailed fingers. "It's a small world, n'est-ce pas, Detective?"

He smiled. "Did she..."

"Did *she* blackmail him? I couldn't say for sure, but Carl Jr. said that she'd pitched a fit when he dumped her in his clumsy German way. Said she'd cry 'rape' if he didn't come back to her. She was frightfully delusional."

"So he paid her off and called it blackmail? Then he suggested she work for his *mother*?"

"No, actually his *mother* paid off Sylvia Arno and his *mother* suggested she come to work for her." She paused for effect. "You look shocked, Detective. Have I shocked you?"

"I am surprised. Why would Ethel Weinrich want that particular woman, a blackmailer no less, to work for her, to live in her house?"

"How better to keep an eye on her? And she certainly could control her, make her do anything... If you ask me there was always something strange about Ethel Weinrich. Something not quite kosher."

"What do you mean?"

"I don't know...She was just strange. It was almost like she wanted people to laugh at her, but then she was surprised when they did."

"Was she a lesbian?"

"Oh that's a good one!" Ellen drawled. "Where in the world did you hear that?"

"It came up during our investigation. So you don't think that was the case?"

"Oh, Detective, *please*. Women like Ethel Weinrich aren't interested in sex period—men, women, whatever. You can forget that angle. In my experience it's usually just name-calling anyway...You know—people used to throw that appellation around in reference to Page Hawthorne—and see how *ridiculous* that turned out to be!"

Ellen laughed shrilly and leaned toward Merton, her dark hair falling forward in a way she obviously intended to be alluring. "Who does Sylvia Arno see now?" he asked, persevering. "Does she 'date' anyone? Have a boyfriend?"

"Now, Detective, how would I know?" she said, her hand fluttering through the air again. "We're not exactly in the same social circle. But if I had to guess, I'd say that she probably still holds a candle for Carl Jr. Why else would she stay in that old museum taking care of that dominating old cow?"

He thought about that for a moment. "Can I ask you one more question?"

"Fire away," said Ellen.

"What do you know about the headmaster out at Rochester-Bingham, Buzz Pinchot?"

Ellen's eyes momentarily brightened. "Thurgood—or Goody as his girlfriends call him? I'm afraid I've been negligent there...I mean I don't know him personally yet."

"How do you mean 'girlfriends'?"

"You know what I mean, Detective. On a scale of one to ten, he's a good solid 7, or so I've heard."

"As a headmaster doesn't he need to be above suspicion?"

"No, that was Caesar's *wife*, and believe me, she *is*." Ellen sighed again at the detective's apparent lack of understanding. "Listen, honey, don't you know that no matter how many women they may put on the board out there, it's still always going to be an old-boy network? They're willing to avert their eyes as long as the dollars continue to flow in, and Thurgood is one hell of a fundraiser.

They say he'll do *anything* for a good gift." Merton shook his head. "Come on, think about it. Have you met Mary Farrell—pronounce that as one word now—Isn't she just the boring little Georgia peach pit?"

"She seemed like a nice lady."

"Oh, that's right." She slid closer to Merton until she was next to him. "I keep forgetting you like nice."

"What about George Crabtree?" he said ignoring her. "Do you think he killed himself?"

She stared at him. "You talked to Mason, didn't you? She says never in a million years. She would know. I think they were in love, deeply in love."

He smiled. "Deeply in love," he repeated.

She arched an eyebrow. "Yes," she said. "Don't you believe

we can fall in love in Middle Essex? It happens sometimes." Her left hand drifted from his shoulder to his face and her fingertips fluttered across his cheek like a moth. "Are you such a cynic now? Why don't you tell me all about your bad experience in Middle Essex love. I'll be your confessor. Tell me everything."

He brushed her hand away. "Maybe another time," he said, leaning forward and setting his hands on his knees as if to push himself up.

But Ellen brought her right hand around and pushed his chest back against the couch. "Don't put me off, Detective. We still have so much to talk about. I won't have it." Then, still holding him down with her right hand, she swung herself up and onto his lap. The weight of her body pressing down on her hand inhibited his movement. The next thing he knew she was straddling him and she had clamped her mouth over his like a succubus.

He pulled away and grabbed her hands. "No," he said.

"Yes," she replied, yanking her hands back. She pulled off her robe. Her skin was shiny and the color of Ritz crackers. She smelled vaguely of Bay Rum.

"Ms. Chevalier," he said, irritation clinging to each syllable. He leaned against her, pushing, but she was surprisingly strong and she had gravity on her side.

Up on her knees, she breathed rapidly. "Detective want to be bad?"

He had half-expected her to pull some such antic, but even so, the situation now was ludicrous and unreal. A sound escaped him, a frustrated growl, and hung in the air. He reached for her shoulders, but she leaned back moaning, her hands at his belt buckle. Then she swooped forward once again, and balancing on her knees above him, leaned down to kiss him. He pulled his face sideways away from her lips and her probing tongue, which she then stuck in his ear. Finally he grabbed her hands away from his pants, pushed with all his strength and stood up.

He looked down at the disheveled woman at his feet. She had narrowly missed the glass table and was now wedged unglamorously between it and the sofa. She lifted one arm to him. Ignoring her, he bent over and picked up his notebook and pen and put them in his pocket.

"Help me," she whispered, giving it all she had, her arm still hanging in the air. When he continued to ignore her, she sat up, but made no attempt to cover herself. She tucked her ankles underneath her buttocks and leaned on the glass table.

He bent down again and picked up her robe and tossed it to her. "Does that act ever actually work for you?" he asked.

She took a big drink, then laughed and put her face on her arms.

He looked at her. "I'm sorry if you misunderstood my intentions. Now put that robe on."

She giggled some more, then looked up, her eyes cold. "There was no misunderstanding. You knew what I wanted when you came over here. You just got scared, didn't you, Mr. Detective?" She reached for the robe and slowly, grudgingly, put it on.

"I came here for information. That's all. I appreciate your talking to me, and if that helps us catch a murderer, I hope you will feel a sense of satisfaction."

"A sense of satisfaction! What a laugh," said Ellen throwing her head back. She laughed for a few moments to illustrate her point, then stopped abruptly, raising blank eyes. "And where do you find your 'sense of satisfaction' these days I wonder? After a hard day of crime-fighting where do you go? To your sparsely furnished condo to read some poetry? Or to a bar? A sports bar maybe? Where you can mingle with your peers."

"You read me like a book," he said.

She stood up. "You're not the cynical creature you pretend to be," she said, crossing her arms. "No, I know. You're back with Sally's sister." She paused, waiting for some acknowledgement in his eyes. He gave it to her and she smiled. "And the worst part is, you *are* in love, aren't you?"

"You must have me confused with someone else."

"I believe there are witnesses." She narrowed her eyes menacingly. "You are a deluded creature and I pity you."

Merton bowed slightly. "If it helps you to pity me, go ahead."

Ellen took a step toward him and bent her head back. Her eyelashes fluttered as her hands fumbled with his belt. "Goodnight, Ms. Chevalier," he said stepping away from her. She dropped to her knees in front of him, her hands still at his belt, and he pushed her away. He looked around the room, at the open blinds on the huge dark windows. "What's going on here?"

"Evidently nothing," she said reaching for her glass on the table. "We're finished. Now get out."

The glass was empty and, when she looked up, he was gone.

LEAVEN OF MALICE

Chapter 43

The little house was aglow with lights, inviting him in, but he sat in his truck in the street, waiting. He waited for a long time, until finally he realized that nothing was going to change how he felt. Maybe Ellen Chevalier was right. Maybe he was a deluded creature worthy of pity.

He closed his eyes and wondered if he had learned anything pertinent enough to the case to make such self-disgust worthwhile. Sylvia Arno had conspired 15 years ago to blackmail Carl Jr. His mother had paid her off, then hired her to be her personal secretary, fully cognizant of Arno's complicity with her son. Ellen Chevalier rejected as absurd the suggestion that Ethel was a lesbian and she did not know whether Sylvia Arno had a boyfriend. She had heard that Buzz Pinchot was a lady's man. His fundraising skills were legendary—he would do anything for a good gift. She agreed with her friend Mason Holt that George Crabtree's death was no suicide. She thought they were 'in love,' although he had no idea what that meant to her. She further believed that he, Roy Merton (although supposedly in love with someone else), would sleep with her given the opportunity and that satisfaction, other than sexual, was illusory. To think otherwise was delusional.

Roy placed his fingers on his temples and pressed. Suddenly he felt as if he might suffocate, as George Crabtree had suffocated the night before, choking on his own sin, unrepentant. He shouldn't be here. Why had he driven here after leaving Ellen Chevalier's house anyway? Who was he kidding? He was overreacting—he hadn't actually done anything. He certainly didn't want to explain any of this to Page.

He looked at the house, remembering another night when he had sat in his truck debating what to do. She didn't want to get married, but he was pretty sure she'd take him back on her terms. That night he had drifted into sleep in an alcohol haze, waking to the woodpecker tapping of a childish hand. He had opened his eyes on Walter, his hands on his hips, his brown eyes squinting in the morning sun. What the hell are you doing here? the boy had demanded belligerently. Stalking my mother? He had smiled for the first time in four days, saying no, but he would like to talk to her. Well, too damn bad he had been told. She's got to take us to school. Tell her I'm here he had said and watch your language while you're at it. He had watched them drive off to school and then watched her return and put the car in the garage and come out the front door and down to his truck. Stalking me? she had said and he had smiled for the second time. They had gone inside together and she had made him a large breakfast and watched him eat it.

Remembering how they had made up, he momentarily considered going inside, but the truth was, that reconciliation had ended badly. They had argued again and he had said terrible things he couldn't take back. He cringed even now thinking about it. He hadn't seen her again for months, not even by chance. So seeing her at home the night before and then at Sally's party, touching her, had unsettled him more than he liked to admit. That was why he found himself sitting in a car in front of her house. But he was behaving like a kid. What did it matter if he had gone over to Ellen Chevalier's house and she had acted like an idiot? He didn't owe Page anything, certainly not an explanation. She had made that clear to him. That was the way she wanted it.

It was time to go home, back to his condo with the TV and the one comfortable chair. Back to a refrigerator filled with beer and frozen dinners. He started the truck and slowly pulled out of the cul-de-sac.

At home he bent to examine the aging pile of mail under the door slot. Nothing even remotely interesting. He stopped in the kitchen and opened the refrigerator. He contemplated its contents, which were minimal. He took a beer and headed into his bedroom. He set the beer on his dresser and pulled off his tie and his Brooks Brothers suit jacket, which he tossed into a corner. Then he unbuttoned his shirt and took it off. It followed the jacket to the corner, as did his pants. He would take them to the cleaners tomorrow. He stepped into the jeans that were folded over the back of the desk chair. Then he picked up his beer and went back to the living room.

He lowered himself onto the black leather chair and set the beer on a pile of books next to it. He felt around and found the remote and turned on the television. It didn't take long to find a black and white movie and he put down the remote and picked up the beer and took a long drink. He couldn't help her. He couldn't help the boys. Not the way things were. He looked at the couple on the screen. It was Olivia de Havilland and Errol Flynn with long hair and an army uniform. He was Custer, and she was saying goodbye to him.

Chapter 44

After awhile she began to feel cold. She pulled her robe tight and went to the bar where she poured herself a tall glass of amber liquid which she sipped as she circled back to the leather couch. She put the drink down carefully on the glass table and picked up the phone and dialed a series of numbers. "Hello," she said in reply to another voice. "It's done."

"Good girl. You always get your man, don't you?"

"Me and the Royal Canadian Mounted Police."

"It didn't take long. I expected he'd need more persuading."

"No persuasion, but he isn't much for foreplay."

"Son of a bitch." The other voice laughed good-naturedly. "I hope it wasn't disappointing for you."

"I'm used to disappointment."

"You *did* get him to…"

She sighed. "The pictures will tell the story."

"Good. I can't wait to see them…In the meantime I could come over…"

"I don't think so. I'm tired. I think I'll just have another drink and read by the fire."

The other voice whooped. "You kill me. You're sure you don't want me to…?"

"I'm sure."

"All right, if that's what you want."

"I didn't say *that*," she said taking a sip. She rattled the ice cubes. "Our detective seemed quite interested in Buzz Pinchot. What do you think that was all about?"

"Buzz? I don't know."

"Well, he wondered if Ethel was a lesbian—so we know they're way off track."

"Grasping at straws."

"Yes, well, I'm tired. Goodnight." She returned the phone to its cradle without waiting for a response and swirled the amber liquid in her glass and thought of a pair of eyes that were nearly the same color. She smiled and felt much better.

Chapter 45

"You're an idiot. You know that?" Vesba crossed her arms across her ample chest and glared, making it clear that she did not for one moment believe her partner. "You're a goddam jackass. Jesus Christ."

"All right," said Merton slamming his chair to the ground noisily so that several heads around the room turned. "Everyone's disappointed with Roy. But we can move ahead with the case today, can't we? We've got something solid to move on..."

"Maybe...I suppose so," she said slowing down. "Where do you want to start? Shall we go talk to Sylvia Arno?"

"Not yet. Let's pay Carl Jr. a visit. Get him to substantiate Ms. Chevalier's statement."

Vesba grunted in agreement and shrugged. "Oh, by the way, I called that development guy last night, that Jack Skokie."

"Did you find anything out?"

She shrugged again. "Skokie said he was fired by Pinchot because the big hitters weren't lining up fast enough to please him. He was getting worried about the capital campaign even though Skokie says there was never anything to worry about. But Pinchot was impatient; he wanted that administration building up and built. He said he could do better himself without paying big bucks to a so-called professional. So Skokie got fired, even though, he says, teachers were screwing students, he was the one who got fired."

"So it was common knowledge about Weinrich's daughter and that Bunting character?"

"I don't know about common knowledge, but this Skokie knew. He said one day some woman, the wife of some teacher, showed up with her two kids and started ranting and raving at some other female teacher in her classroom about having an affair with her husband…"

"A regular soap opera."

"Well, according to this Skokie, there was a lot of crap hitting the fan, but he got tanked because Pinchot was preoccupied with fundraising and Pinchot had it out for him. I must admit, he did seem to be eating a steady diet of sour grapes."

"You don't think *he* had anything to do with…"

"Unfortunately, no. He was out of town at some conference. He did say that Pinchot had always handled Mrs. Weinrich personal, that he never let anyone else near her."

"What about Crabtree? Pinchot said Crabtree went over to her house, that he…"

"I know. I know. I'm just telling you what he said."

He nodded. "We better get a move on."

They stood up together and began to put on their jackets. As Vesba bent to take her handbag out of her bottom file drawer she caught the eye of the station receptionist. "Merton," she said pointing.

"Call on one," he said. "Let me get this." He picked up the phone and pressed a button. "Merton here," he said. "*Page?*" He flicked his eyes at his partner and turned his back to her. "Slow down…Sure. Don't worry. Fifteen minutes." He hung up. He looked at Vesba. "That was Page Hawthorne. She said I better come right over."

Chapter 46

Page was in the living room, sitting in a wing chair by the fire. She was still wearing her black running tights and an old gray sweatshirt with WILLIAMS COLLEGE in purple letters across the front. She was not smiling. When the doorbell rang, she got up and walked to the door. "What's she doing here?" she said when she opened it.

"We're working today," said Merton, as if that explained everything.

"Well, you might want to have her wait in the car," said Page, crossing her arms.

Vesba groaned. "I'm not waiting in the car. Let's just go," she said hitting her partner in the arm.

"What is it you want me to see?" asked Merton.

"In here," said Page turning.

The two detectives followed her into the living room. Spread out on the coffee table were a dozen 4" x 6" photographs. Merton's eyes did not settle on the photographs immediately. He looked at Page who had turned to the fire.

"Jesus," mumbled Vesba.

"They were delivered by courier about half an hour ago," Page said. "I called you right away."

"Which courier company?" asked Vesba, reaching for her pen and pad.

"Express, I think," said Page calmly. "But you don't need to trace it. There was a personal note with the pictures, signed and everything." She turned to the wing chair and picked up a small manila envelope, which she handed to Vesba.

Merton had taken a seat on the sofa and was staring at the pictures. His hands hung limply over his knees. Vesba joined him on the couch and began picking them up, one at a time, to study them.

She whistled once or twice, but that was all.

"Can I see the note, please," he said extending his hand. Vesba put the envelope in his hand and went back to studying the photos. He opened the envelope and pulled out a piece of fancy bond paper, ivory with an engraved monogram in gray block letters, WCMcH. He began to read the handwritten note slowly out loud.

> Dear Page,
> The dog has returned to his vomit. Have you learned your lesson yet?
>   Yours, Willis McHugh

Merton handed the note to his partner who had her hand out.

"You were set up," Page said as she sat down. "Big Time."

He nodded. "I was set up."

"Whoever took these was a pro," said Vesba. "Look at the angle on this one here, where Ms. Chevalier is on the floor with her arm raised. See her hand? It looks like..."

"Shut up, Leona," he said, snatching the photo away. He scanned the photos once again and then began to gather them together quickly into a pile like a deck of cards. Then he put them on the table and stared at his folded hands. No one said anything for a while.

"Does anybody else think there's a coincidence here?" said Page softly. "I mean with this being the second set of...photos that have turned up in the past few days? Or is this just the new game they're playing in Middle Essex?"

Merton shrugged. "The Weinrich girl? This doesn't have anything to do with that. It's just Willis McHugh being an asshole..."

"Well, why don't you just throw them into the fire then," said Page in a voice edged with impatience.

He looked up at a bird on the fabric of the chair above Page's head. "What?" he asked, his voice husky.

"*Burn* them."

"They're evidence," said Vesba.

"*Evidence of what?*" she said leaning forward.

Merton made a noise in the back of his throat and stood up.

Vesba cleared her throat. "So we have to ask ourselves, is it interesting that Willis and Ellen are working together?" she asked, watching her partner's back. "And we have to answer, what else did she have to do last night?" Vesba flipped a hand in the air. "Maybe the nympho actually thought she'd get lucky...Probably McHugh has something on *her* and...you get the idea."

"And now he's got something on me?"

"It isn't much," said Vesba, picking up a photo. "It's obvious she didn't get you into bed, although she seems to have been trying pretty hard." She started to cackle, but stopped when she caught a glimpse of her partner staring at Page who was leaning forward now on her knees staring at the table. She picked up the photos and patted them into a neat pile and put them into her purse. Merton turned and put out his hand. She reopened her purse and took out the photos and handed them to her partner who shoved them into the inside pocket of his jacket. She cracked her knuckles. "You're free, white and 21 and can damn well do what you want on a Sunday night. Why should anyone care?"

"Anyone wouldn't care," said Page. "He sent them to *me*. It's because we were together, he saw us up in Sally's study."

"Well, then," said Vesba. "He reacted the same way I did when I heard you two were together. Disbelief followed by nausea." She stared at Page and crossed her legs with some difficulty.

Merton turned to his partner. "Leona," he said. "Go wait in the car." When she didn't immediately respond, he repeated the command leaving no doubt about his meaning.

Grudgingly Vesba got to her feet. "I'll wait three minutes and then I'm out of here."

"Fine," he said.

When she heard the front door close, Page stood up. Roy shook his head, unsmiling. "I'm sorry you had to see these."

She crossed her arms. "When did this happen anyway?"

"Last night. She called about six. Leona was on her way home. I figured she was up to something, but I thought I could handle it. I thought it might be worth the trouble." He looked at Page. "Why do you ask?"

"You told me you saw her on Saturday night. I wondered if you..."

"What?" he asked, staring.

"I wondered if...you went home with her."

He shook his head slowly. "You think I sent you home with Billy so I could take *her* home?" He stood up; she stepped back. "Those pictures are fakes. You know that."

"I know," she said. "I'm sorry. I've just been sitting here thinking. Thinking too much."

"And what have you been thinking?" He stepped to her side and she turned away and faced the mantel. He looked down at her golden head and breathed in the scent of soap and shampoo mixed with the slight smell of sweat from her morning walk. "Thinking about old Roy?" he said, folding his arms in front of his chest. "Wondering about the women I must have now that I've undoubtedly gone back to my wild bachelor ways? Thinking, gee, maybe he didn't go home and suffer some more." He was suddenly angry. "A funny thing happened last night, Page, something that ought to really amuse you. I drove over here after my brief encounter with Ellen Chevalier. I'm not really sure why and, of course, I didn't come in. I knew better than to do that. I just sat in the truck and then I went home and took off those clothes and fell asleep watching an old movie. And I had a dream. I was happy in the dream, so happy. We had a child, a little girl. I was with her at the beach, a long stretch of beach, just walking. I was careful to walk slowly and always to hold her little hand. Then we stopped and I turned to look at something down the beach and I dropped her hand. It was only for a second. When I turned back to her, she was gone. Only her tiny shoes were left on the sand. I was overcome with horror, panic. I looked everywhere, even wading into the ocean, but I couldn't find her. Finally I forced myself to wake up. I was relieved that it was just a dream."

He thought he saw her wince very slightly and he was inwardly satisfied when she put both hands on the mantel, steadying herself. He could hear her taking quick, shallow breaths.

He took the pictures out of his pocket and placed them on the mantel. "For the moon never beams without bringing me dreams," he said. After a while he checked his watch. Then he turned and left the house.

She knelt and placed the pile gingerly between two burning logs, where they caught fire and began to curl and blaze. She did not move until all the photos were ash.

Chapter 47

Vesba put her car in gear and craned her neck to scan the road as she backed down the driveway. In the street she braked too abruptly, shifted with unnecessary vehemence and tore off into the road that led out of Rockville after spinning her tires on the scattered gravel beneath them. Her partner did not seem to notice as he stared out the side window, and he only turned his head slightly when she suddenly slammed on the brakes. "Don't you want to comment on what went on in there?" she said raising her hands off the steering wheel in an exaggerated gesture of confusion. "Don't you have anything to say?"

"No," he said calmly. "We're going downtown to see Carl Jr. What are we waiting for?"

"Okay," said Vesba, but she did not take her foot off the brakes. "You don't want to go there. I can understand that." She hesitated. "But I was thinking about something I said in there, about why Ellen Chevalier would play along with McHugh. I said that the mayor maybe has something on her—something he can hold over her head to make her do things. And I've been thinking—you know—that's the way he operates. He takes pictures, gathers info, threatens people. Maybe he had something on Crabtree..."

"I told Page it had nothing to do with those pictures of the Weinrich girl..."

"Yeah, but...what if it did?" She glanced at him.

He was staring at her. "Maybe Mrs. Weinrich really did have something on the mayor? Maybe all those journal entries added up to something. Could it be McHugh who's working with Arno?" asked Merton. "God, if we could nail the bastard..."

"First, we've got to get Arno to talk," said Vesba.

"Do you think the pictures...of me...could Sylvia Arno have taken them?"

"Those pictures were taken by a professional," she said slowly. "She doesn't really strike me as the type."

He took a deep breath. "I don't think Page will try to respond to McHugh." He turned to her as if for reassurance. "She could step right in the middle of something."

"*She* won't do anything now," she said firmly. "No way. She showed you the pictures and now she's going to sit in that chair and stew, if she even stews. Nothing's going to happen to Page in that house."

He ran his fingers through his hair and took another deep breath.

"I'm right," she said, turning away. She looked out the window. "You know I am."

He didn't say anything, but she felt him turn toward her. When she turned her head back, he was staring at her, and she narrowed her eyes instinctively to counter their effect.

"What?" she said.

"Don't ever talk to Page like that again."

She stared back, biting her tongue. He was serious. She swallowed hard. "Okay," she said slowly.

Finally he looked away.

She hesitated, but she couldn't stop herself. "But why would I even see her again?" she said. She swallowed hard. Her mouth felt unnaturally dry. She wished she had a bottle of water. "We don't need to have anything more to do with her. She isn't part of this investigation. As far as I'm concerned, I never saw those pictures."

He was still looking out the side window and she turned and fixed her gaze on the windshield. "You've got to forget her," she said. "You're 'vomit' in their eyes." She waited, but he wasn't going to say anything; he was finished.

"Fine then," she said, and no longer hesitating, she spun her tires, and in a shower of gravel, tore away from the curb.

Chapter 48

The door closed quietly behind the detectives as the secretary backed out of the office. Carl Weinrich, Jr. gazed out the window at the city skyline, not yet acknowledging his visitors. The detectives waited as the grandfather clock in the corner audibly counted the moments and then Leona Vesba cleared her throat noisily and pulled a client chair backwards with a sudden, violent jerk.

Carl Jr. turned around. He did not smile, but held his hand out in a gesture suggesting they sit down as he himself pulled back his desk chair and lowered his bulk into it with a resounding thump. The detectives sat down and exchanged glances.

"Detectives," said Carl Jr. too loudly. "How can I help you today?"

"Mr. Weinrich," began Vesba. "I'll come right to the point of our visit. We've been told that you had an affair 15 years ago with a paralegal in this office..."

"Fifteen years ago?" interrupted Carl Jr. He smiled but his hands gripped the arms of his chair. "I hope you don't expect me to remember every little paralegal I've dallied with since..."

"Her name was Sylvia Arno," said Vesba, ignoring his interruption. "She tried to blackmail you...then she went to work for your mother."

Carl Jr. now resembled an eggplant and he appeared to inflate in his chair. His blue eyes bulged. He seemed to struggle inwardly, as if trying to decide whether to tell the truth. "Where did you hear such a ridiculous story?" he gasped.

"Ridiculous maybe," said Merton. "But we know it's true."

Carl. Jr. expelled air and sank back into his chair. The carotid artery in his neck throbbed visibly. He did not look at them but stared at his flattened right hand which lay palm down on the blotter. "I made a mistake. She wasn't exactly a kid, but she was inexperienced...Let me tell you, though, when she got angry, she was no pushover. I found that out. When she finally understood that she couldn't have me, she wanted money. My wife was pregnant...I couldn't...I had to go to my mother. She was remarkably understanding, as if somehow she had been expecting me to. She paid Sylvia off and *she* offered her the job at home. It was *her* idea. I know that sounds crazy—I thought so at the time—but I never questioned my mother's decisions, much less her motives. I learned that at an early age...I don't know anything else about it. I kept out of it...I turned my face to the wall...I always thought they deserved each other."

"What does that mean?" asked Vesba.

"It means they were both champion grudge holders. For all I know they shared voodoo dolls and stuck pins in them. They seemed to get along. They went to Europe together several times. My mother was very generous with her." Carl Jr. stopped suddenly and looked first at Vesba and then to Merton. "You don't think? You don't think..."

"We think a lot of things. We think all the time," said Vesba scooting forward in her chair. "I think Warren Beatty is a hot ticket, but I don't think he ought to run for president."

Carl Jr. stared. Then he remembered that his mouth was open and he closed it. His teeth made a chopping noise when he did so.

"Okay, Mr. Weinrich," said Vesba. "Tell us about your relationship with Sylvia Arno since she moved in with your mother and became her secretary."

He sighed heavily and leaned further back in his chair. "Sylvia Arno and I have stayed in touch over the years."

"Stayed in touch?" interrupted Vesba. "What does that mean—stayed in touch—were you pen pals?"

"No," said Carl Jr. hesitating. "We stayed in touch."

"What? Spell it out for me. You had sex from time to time?" she asked impatiently.

"Yes. My mother never knew."

"You assume your mother never knew," said Merton. "I wouldn't be too sure."

"Why do you say that?" asked Carl Jr. "Do you know something?"

Merton ignored his question and asked his own. "Did you know that your mother had changed her will again? That the school was back in?"

"I didn't until David Whittier told me the other day—after my mother was...after she died."

"Sylvia Arno didn't tell you?" asked Vesba.

"Sylvia knew?"

The detectives exchanged glances. "Were you involved in this latest blackmail attempt?" asked Merton.

Carl Jr. looked from one detective to the other, his watery blue eyes beseeching them. He picked up a paper clip and began to unfold it. "I was involved, but it was all *her* idea. She saw the kids—what they were doing. She told me it would be easy to take pictures..."

"Of your own daughter?" asked Vesba, an edge of disgust creeping into her voice.

"Yes...She said it would be easy to squeeze some money out of my mother...She knew I needed money...These casinos in town—I've had a hell of a time...And all the while there's my mother sitting up there on her pile of money, judging me. It's so unfair!"

"Sure it is," said Vesba glancing again at her partner. "Why didn't you just ask her for the money?"

"I couldn't just ask her for it...Not again...You can see my predicament."

"Oh, sure," said Vesba, almost spitting. "But, tell us, what was Ms. Arno going to get out of this?"

"Sylvia?" said Carl Jr. who was poking his hand with the sharp end of the paper clip. "She was helping me, because...she loves me. She always has."

Vesba rolled her eyes over to Merton, but he was gazing at his own hands in his lap and did not look up. "*She loves you*? That's why she's been living with your mother all these years? So she can be close to you—sort of—and occasionally have sex with you and help you, when the need arises, to blackmail your mother. I see."

"I never really gave it much thought. I know it must sound..."

"No, sir, I don't think you do know how it sounds...But that doesn't matter. The question I have now is this: Is that all you and Ms. Arno cooked up together? Blackmail?"

Yes, Detective," said Carl Jr. "Of course, it is."

"Maybe you did find out about the will, that your slice of Mommy's pie was going to be smaller than expected. Maybe you hatched a new plan, a little plan involving murder?"

"Oh, no!" said Carl Jr. breathlessly, still poking the palm of his hand. "You can't think that! My own *mother*—you can't be serious."

"You didn't draw the line at photographing your own daughter," said Vesba, spitting again.

"That was different! I was desperate! I was…"

"Desperate for money. Yes, we understand that, only now you're asking us to believe you weren't desperate enough to kill."

"Yes! I mean no!" whined Carl Jr. "Never. I didn't even know about the will. I swear…if I had, I'd have known she'd eventually change it back—like she always did. She was just mad at me about the blackmail…"

"So you lied," said Merton looking up suddenly. "You lied about the day the pictures were delivered."

"Yes," said Carl Jr., his eyes like blue saucers. Little beads of perspiration had formed on his upper lip and he sucked it in. He looked down. "Sylvia said to—so the two things, the blackmail and the murder, wouldn't be connected. Not that we were involved or anything…"

"Sylvia thinks of everything," said Vesba.

"Yes," said Carl Jr., throwing down the paper clip and picking up a tissue from a leather holder on his desk. He held the tissue to his bleeding palm and looked at Vesba who was leaning forward, resting her forearms on the desk. "Sylvia thinks of everything."

Merton stood up abruptly and extended his hand, then pulled it back. "Thank you for your time. We'll be back in touch soon."

"Do I need a lawyer?" asked Carl Jr.

"You *are* a lawyer," said Vesba. "What do you think?" She picked up her handbag and smiled amiably at the confused man behind the desk. Then she turned and followed Merton out the door, skipping to catch up with him as he strode through the stately outer offices and out to the hallway where the elevator was located. He said nothing, but stared at the marble floor and waited for the elevator to travel up to their floor. She crossed her arms in front of her chest, straining the seams that held the sleeves to her jacket. She said nothing and they traveled in silence to the lobby.

In the split second when she stepped off the elevator and saw the small, trim figure with the familiar dark blonde hair falling in smooth sheets to her shoulders, before her chubby foot encased in turquoise vinyl even hit the marble floor, Vesba had assessed the situation, judging the moment, and made a decision. She gripped the arm of her distracted partner and guided him in the opposite direction, away from the woman in black who waited at the other end of the lobby. They had work to do. There was time enough for him to find out that Page was going to see a lawyer.

Chapter 49

In Vesba's car Merton swung his arm around the top of the seat. He considered his partner for a moment, focusing on her dangling gold earrings, which were so heavy, they stretched her earlobes. He thought of Page's ears, touchingly small and perfect, and how he had studied them when he had first known her, sitting in her tiny office at the church, willing her to turn around, to notice him.

His partner turned around and faced him, her earrings swinging. "What do we do now?" she asked. "Back to Middle Essex?"

He exhaled and fought to concentrate. "I say we call the captain, explain what we've got. Say we need a warrant to search Ms. Arno's room at the house. Send a team out—maybe they'll turn up something. In the meantime, we'll bring her down to the station. We'll talk about Carl Jr."

"Get her to tell us who was cooking the pop tarts."

"Yes."

"It sounds like a plan to me."

Chapter 50

David Whittier embraced Page fondly and then held her at arms length to look at her. She regarded him with affection and was glad to see he had not changed much since their last encounter. At age 70, his blue eyes were clear and boyish and his straight gray hair needed a trim as always. His nose was just big enough not to look too feminine. His lips stretched into a wide, pleasing smile and exposed his own teeth. He was glad to see her.

"Ah, Page," he said. "What a nice surprise for a dull Monday! What brings you down here? No trouble at home I hope?"

"No," she said returning his grin. "No trouble. I came down to speak to Renzi Stark."

"Renzi?" he asked, a note of suspicion coloring the question.

She noted the cloud that came over his eyes. "Yes. I just need to ask him something. It won't take a minute."

"Fine. I know someone else takes care of your taxes…Bernie Straub, isn't it?"

"Yes," she said. "Renzi's a friend. It's personal."

"Oh?" said David Whittier, the slight air of suspicion still lying limply on the surface of his voice.

"I just thought I'd stop by while I was here to say hello to you."

"I'm so glad you did," he said brightening. "I don't get to see my goddaughter nearly enough. We should have lunch. Are you busy today?"

"Yes, as a matter of fact. I have an appointment."

"That's a shame," he said meaning it. "I see Sally, but I never seem to see you."

Page smiled but made no comment.

"I don't believe I even saw you at her party the other night.

You were there, of course."

"Of course," she said, her smile beginning to fade. "With Billy Custer."

"Ah, Billy. When are you two going to get married? Everyone knows you're perfect for each other. We're all far too busy nowadays. You and Gwen and I will have to have dinner soon. Yes, and Billy, the next time he's in town."

It was time to go. She recognized the code and the tone of dismissal. She smiled again and offered her cheek to be kissed. Her godfather smiled, then dropped his face and retreated to his desk, already thinking of something else.

Renzi Stark's secretary, whom he shared with two other attorneys, buzzed him and he appeared momentarily at her desk, hand extended to Page.

"Hello! Good to see you, Page!" He shook her hand and touched her elbow, directing her to his office. "Please, come this way."

They sat down and settled themselves. Renzi chose the other client chair, so they faced each other at a slight angle. He searched her face for some clue as to why she was sitting in his office. "Is everything all right?" he asked finally.

"Oh yes," she said, returning his gaze. She had not seen Renzi Stark since he had graduated from high school. Had she attended his wedding? Certainly she would remember that, wouldn't she? A wedding, two children, time had rolled by. She scanned his office, feeling sick and sad.

"What is it then?" Stark asked. "What can I do for you?"

"Oh, I just wanted to ask you something."

"Fire away then," he said, his smile free of doubt and uncertainty.

"Renzi," Page began. "Do you ever read *Forward Day by Day*?"

Doubt and uncertainty returned to Renzi Stark's face. "Well, no, I can't say that I do...with any regularity at least."

Page smiled. "Well, I do, and a few weeks ago the scripture was from I Kings—the story of Ahab and Jezebel."

"I'm afraid I don't...I'm not..."

Page pulled a piece of paper out of her purse and handed it to him. "If you don't mind, please read verses 1-16. There," she said pointing.

He did as she asked, and when he was finished, he looked up.

"I'm sorry. I'm still confused."

She took the paper from his outstretched hand. "It's a story about corruption...the corruption of power." Page looked down at the paper in her hand and read aloud, "*Jezebel said to Ahab, Arise, take possession of the vineyard of Naboth the Jezreelite, which he refused to give thee for money.*" She looked at Stark. "It just got me thinking, you know, and wondering about those two little houses that used to stand between the two schools, Rochester Hall and Bingham. I noticed the last time I drove down Beasley Road that they're gone. I suppose they were torn down to make room for the new administration building."

"Yes," he said. "That's right."

"Who owned those two houses?" asked Page, leaning slightly forward in her chair, her bright amber eyes wide.

Stark swallowed. "I believe both houses were owned by...Willis McHugh."

Page leaned back. "I thought I'd heard that," she said quietly. "But who owned them before the mayor?"

"I'm not sure," said Stark. "But I could find out."

"I suppose the school bought the property from McHugh?"

"Yes. The school paid around a million dollars for both properties."

"And how much did he pay for them I wonder?"

"I could find that out too." He folded his hands in his lap. He looked at Page, concern filling his eyes. "But what, may I ask, are you planning to do with this information—if I give it to you? McHugh can be a dangerous man to cross."

"I know."

"Everything was done legally."

"I'm sure of it...but Willis is in public office. Sometimes just the appearance or suggestion of impropriety is enough to..."

"To what, Page? He could hurt you.."

"He already has," said Page, steeling herself. Unexpected kindness always disabled her resolve. "I would turn the other cheek, but he doesn't respect that. He despises what he perceives to be weakness. They all do. They want to squash it. I won't be squashed."

"I don't understand," said Stark.

"You don't need to. I just need the facts concerning those real estate transactions. That's all I want from you, Renzi."

He nodded and stared across his desk at the window behind it. "Sometimes I wonder why I stay in this town," he said. "But I guess it's no different anywhere else. I'll get the information you need."

"Renzi," said Page, closing her eyes and exhaling slowly. "I don't think he'll be able to trace this back to you, but..."

"Don't worry. It doesn't matter. Gussie told me what you said to her about my job. You were right."

"Was I?"

"Yes. We've talked about it before."

Page put her hand on his for a moment. "Everything will work out, Renzi."

"I know."

"Now do you think you can get the information by 3 o'clock? I need it by 3 o'clock."

"I'll do my best and call you."

"I'll be waiting to hear from you," said Page as she stood up.

Renzi Stark reached out and took her outstretched hand with both of his. "All right," he said. "I'll do what I can."

C.R.COMPTON

Chapter 51

Page Merton climbed into her Volvo full of dread, fear and loathing, the whole nine yards. She put the key in the ignition and started the car. As she strapped on her seat belt and threw her arm back over the seat, she pictured herself swinging into the saddle and the anxious horse underneath her rearing as she backed out of the garage. She paused as the door came down to put Wynonna on the CD player. *To tell the truth, I'm bulletproof,* she sang, *so take your best shot at me.* At the bottom of her driveway, she began to turn left. *Be bold, Little Sister.* At first she didn't even recognize the sound, so preoccupied with her plans was she and so unfamiliar was its metallic trill, but finally she picked up the cell phone in her console and said, "Hello?"

"Page, *where are you?* I've been calling all over the place for hours."

"Sally?"

"Yes, it's Sally. Remember me? Your sister, the one who had a party the other night? I think you were there, but I wouldn't swear to it."

"I'm sorry, Sally. It was a great party…"

"Yes, it was," she interrupted. She took a deep breath and let it out slowly. "Where *are* you, Page? What's all that noise?"

"I'm in my driveway actually. I have an appointment—I was leaving…"

"Good, we can talk on your way there."

"O.K.," Page said shifting the car into park. She turned off the CD player. "Go ahead."

"Listen, what was going on Saturday night—and don't try to tell me nothing. Willis McHugh was…bizarre, and then Roy Merton, of all people, showing up. He said you asked him to come over. Why, Page? I thought you had worked all that out. You're not trying to get back with Roy are you?"

"Would that be such a bad thing?"

Sally waited for Page to continue, but she didn't. "Well, you can't blame me for wondering, considering the very strange phone call from Ellen Chevalier this morning saying..."

"Saying what?" said Page feeling suddenly cold. "Saying I might want to call my little sister because you might be having a bad day." Sally waited again for Page to comment, but when her sister was still silent, she ploughed ahead. "I said what *kind* of a bad day, Ellen, and she played coy and hinted around ...Page, are you still there?"

"Yes, Sally."

"Well, that isn't all, Page. Ellen insinuated that she was with Roy last night, that, as she put it, she 'got the full measure of the man.'"

"He went to her house to ask her some more questions about the Ethel Weinrich case. But nothing happened."

"How do you know that?" pressed Sally. "How do you even know where he was last night? Have you talked to him?"

"Yes. But I don't want to talk about this now, Sally. Not in my car."

"It's not my fault you're in your *car*. This is the best I can do and you've got to listen to me. Now look, I thought you had already faced the hard facts about this guy, Page. Roy is not what you imagined, what you dreamed him to be. He's a man who knows how to manipulate women. He's a pro..."

"Then he can handle Ellen Chevalier, can't he?"

Sally sighed. "He can handle *you*, Page. I'm not so sure you can handle him."

"I don't need to 'handle' him, Sally," she said. "And I don't care what Ellen Chevalier told you. What does it have to do with me anyway? I'm sorry that she will undoubtedly lie to a lot of people, most of them your friends, but so what? I don't care what those people think."

Sally waited for several seconds. "Okay, look, Page, I'm sorry. I shouldn't be butting in, and I would never intentionally hurt your feelings, but Ellen just got me so upset, and then when I couldn't track you down, I...Look, I can't help feeling there's more to this."

"I'll be late. I've got to go now."

"No wait, Page. Where are you going that's so important?"

"I have an appointment."

"Page..." she said and waited, but again there was no response. "Well, when can we talk?"

"I don't know. Tomorrow I guess."

"You'll be home?"

"Where else would I be?"

"Oh, I don't know...Just listen. You know I'm here for you. You can always come here. Phil and I love you, Page. We'll help you if you need help."

"I know, Sally. But I don't need your help. I'll talk to you tomorrow." She pressed the End button. She turned off the phone and put the car into drive, swinging out into the street, hoping that the bones which had been broken might rejoice.

Chapter 52

"Don't you ever clean this place up? This room is filthy, not to mention dark and...really remarkably unpleasant." Sylvia Arno regarded the dreary interrogation room and shuddered.

"You're right, you know," said Vesba perching on the end of the table, which creaked a shrill warning whenever she moved. "A few throw pillows would really brighten up the place." Her partner, who leaned sideways against the green wall, stifled a laugh.

"I'm glad you amuse each other, because I am not laughing," said Sylvia. "Why am I here anyway?"

"Because we need to ask you some more questions," said Vesba.

"You talked to me twice already, both times at the house. Why did I have to come all the way over here this time?"

"They're searching your rooms even as we speak," said Merton turning to face Sylvia. "We wouldn't want to get in their way."

"What?" said Sylvia whose round blue eyes grew suddenly rounder. "I don't understand. Do I need to call my lawyer?"

"And who would your lawyer be now? Certainly not Carl Jr. or anyone, for that matter, at his firm. That wouldn't be considered appropriate...even in Middle Essex," he said.

Sylvia looked down. She looked up. She pursed her lips until it looked as if her lips were missing. She looked sideways.

"We know you were blackmailing Ethel Weinrich," said Merton pulling out a chair and sitting. "Carl Jr. even said it was your idea. It would be an easy way to ring a few million out of his mother. You'd done it before, you could do it again. He needed the money. Why not? But why *now*? After so many years? Why now? That puzzled us...It seemed like it had to have a connection with the murder...but it didn't really, did it? It was just a distraction, a way to get us off the track with Carl Jr., thinking about Carl and a possible motive for killing his mother. And maybe while we were off the track we wouldn't notice something else."

"Carl Jr. won't press charges. He was involved. So there is no blackmail. You can't hold me. You have no evidence of anything else."

"No," said Vesba. "We just want to talk."

"About what?"

"About what they'll find in your rooms," said Vesba.

"What will we find I wonder?" mused Merton.

"You won't find anything in my rooms because there is nothing to find."

"A key to the school maybe?" he said. "So you could sneak in through some dark back door and surprise Mrs. Weinrich, getting her to go down to the lunch room so you could kill her?"

"That's absurd."

"Is it?" said Merton, leaning forward. "Who gave you a key? Who? Maybe it was George Crabtree—who then, conveniently, killed himself out of remorse."

"Or maybe it wasn't Crabtree," suggested Vesba. "But perhaps he figured out who it *was,* and then you had no choice but to kill him, make it look like suicide."

"But who would believe that?" cut in Merton. "George Crabtree feeling remorse? George Crabtree who had so much to live for? George Crabtree who got knocked on the head? Who couldn't drive without his glasses, but was found in his car without them? Who was found wearing his seatbelt—who wears their seatbelt when they're committing suicide?" He stood up slowly and stepped to the window. He tapped the pane, thinking. "No," he said. "No. George Crabtree stumbled on to something, something nasty. Perhaps he underestimated you and your partner—maybe he thought he could blackmail *you?* He always thought he was so much smarter than everyone else, didn't he? That eastern prep school snob? He even looked down his nose at his boss, didn't he? That upstart from Georgia? It must have irked him to have to work for him, to have to follow his orders...But you fixed him, didn't you? You and your partner."

"I don't have the slightest idea what you are talking about. I can't follow a word of it. Not a word."

"Oh, yes you can," said Vesba. "I think you can. You go

ahead and play the poor dumb girl if you want, but here's notice, we aren't falling for it any more. The nun attire, the bun—it's all for show, an act, isn't it? Who were you supposed to be fooling? Mrs. Weinrich? What did she think of your long red nails? And your midnight callers?"

"Midnight callers? You're delusional, Detective," said Sylvia Arno, throwing out her arms in a gesture of exasperation. She sighed deeply, expelling air out her nostrils while she gritted her teeth. "You can think what you want to think, but you don't have *proof* or even a motive. Why would I want to kill Ethel Weinrich? I'm out of a job for god's sake!"

"Yes, that's true enough," said Vesba evenly. "You've lost your job...but according to Mrs. Weinrich's most recent will, you'll be coming into a nice amount of money. She was feeling unusually generous towards you, wasn't she? You and the school."

"So? What does that prove? I'd worked for her for 15 years. I'd been faithful and done just what she wanted all those years. I was *loyal.* She appreciated that. She valued that sort of thing."

"Yes...and she was loyal to you. She valued your opinion. She followed your advice, didn't she?"

"We agreed on things."

"Oh, come now, Ms. Arno," said Merton. "You're being modest now—"

"*You* were pitching, weren't you, Sylvia?" interrupted Vesba. "Mrs. Weinrich was catching. *That's* the way it was. She'd do anything for *you*—Isn't that true?"

"None of this has any bearing on who killed poor Ethel now, does it?" said Sylvia patiently. She looked down at her navy skirt picking imaginary lint from it.

"Maybe it does. Maybe you were getting tired of the situation. Fifteen years is a long time to work for someone who by most accounts was a cranky old bitch," said Vesba. "Maybe you had new prospects."

Sylvia looked up. "You're being absurd again. I devoted myself to Mrs. Weinrich. Why would I want to...Why would I betray her trust? I have no other prospects—I'm nearly 40 years old."

"All the more reason for a change in plan," said Merton.

"Especially if old Carl Jr. had made it clear that you had no prospects with *him*. When did he tell you that?" asked Vesba pressing forward on the table. "A few weeks ago? You had to think fast—or did you?"

"Who's been waiting in the wings, Sylvia? George Crabtree maybe?" He crossed his arms and smiled. "We passed a black Saab driving up to see you just the other day. Did he let himself in the back way? No, probably not. You never liked George, did you? No. That isn't why he came to see you. On the other hand, you had a little soft spot for Renzi Stark—but not quite soft enough as it turned out. No, you could tell the tide was going against Renzi so you threw a little stick of your own into the current about him driving Ethel home. Let's see—who else? There's always been Willis McHugh. Mrs. Weinrich was stirring up the pot there—you knew that. You could have gone over and helped him. He might have been grateful."

"You're crazy," said Sylvia.

"Hardly," said Merton. "We know there was a black Lexus parked outside Crabtree's house on Saturday night for about 45 minutes between 9:30 and 10:15. A nosy neighbor told us that. McHugh drives a black Lexus, Sylvia. Did you know that?"

"Willis McHugh—that's absurd."

"No, not absurd—just incorrect. You're thinking about someone else who drives a black Lexus..."

"We *know* who you were in bed with, Sylvia," shouted Vesba. "We know."

"You're crazy! You're fishing—just fishing! All this is only circumstantial evidence. You can't put me together with anyone! You haven't one shred of evidence to link me with anyone."

Merton returned to the table and leaned on his hands, staring at Sylvia from under his eyebrows. "We have phone records. We know who you called Saturday afternoon after George Crabtree drove away in his black Saab. We know he called you late on Saturday night. And as a matter of fact we have *him*, and he's nervous as hell."

"You're lying."

"He's right outside."

She paused. "He wouldn't say a word."

"You can think that if you want, but you know how it works, Ms. Arno. The first one to talk has a better chance of dealing with the D.A."

Chapter 53

She arrived first. She settled herself on a cement garden bench (In Memory of Gladys Pickerel Benton, class of 1926) and folded her hands, contemplating the idyllic scene before her. The bench upon which she sat was located under a large tree at the top of a hill which sloped gently down to a tiny pond with a tiny dock and three Canadian geese. To the south stretched two hockey fields and to the west, neatly terraced on three levels, were nine tennis courts.

Page calmed herself by repeating snatches of a short psalm: *O Lord, I am not proud...I do not occupy myself with great matters, or with things that are too hard for me. But I still my soul and make it quiet, like a child upon its mother's breast; my soul is quieted within me...*She tried to picture Willis McHugh as a child comforted in his mother's lap. The notion amused her and she laughed out loud and the color came back into her face, so that when the mayor rounded the corner from the south parking lot and caught sight of her, it was Page Hawthorne luminous and empowered and at ease in her body.

McHugh scowled. His bullet head appeared to sprout directly from his shoulders as he trudged up the slight incline to meet Page. She forced herself to smile sweetly. In the distance the distinctive crack of a hockey ball hitting a stick reverberated, carried by the breeze whispering in the branches of the tree above her. "This is quite a tree," she said looking up. "It's a mulberry I guess. I bet it's 150 years old—it's so huge!" She touched the gnarled trunk. "Isn't it beautiful?"

"It's a goddam tree," mumbled McHugh. "A goddam *worthless* tree, not some poem or some painting."

"Oh, I see I've touched a nerve," she said. "I'm sorry. I should thank you for coming, Willis. It was good of you to take the time out of your busy day..."

"I *am* busy, Page, and I don't have time to chat about trees."

"Of course not. I understand. Why don't you sit down?"

He looked down at the bench and considered sitting, but the bench was small. "No," he said turning away. "No. I hope this won't take long."

"No," said Page. She stood up and took a few steps forward toward the crest of the hill where McHugh stood. "Why did you send me those pictures, Willis?"

He turned halfway around. "Did you like them?" he asked grinning suddenly.

"No, not very much."

"Oh, that's too bad! I thought you'd get a big kick out of seeing your brave detective in action. Ellen sure did."

"I hope you rewarded her handsomely."

He erased the grin and pursed his lips. "So you've seen them. What now?"

"I'm not sure. I threw them away, but I suppose there are negatives.

"Negatives! They're digital. They can be all over the Internet in a couple of seconds! If you want them, I think we'll have to think of something you can give me."

"An exchange," she said, straightening her shoulders. "What could I have that you would want?"

"What, indeed," said McHugh looking at her uneasily. "I heard you'd broken up with him, Page. I heard the sucker wanted to get married, and you, for once demonstrating some good judgment, said no. So what happened?"

"Nothing happened," she said.

"Come on. *Something* happened. That wasn't nothing I saw upstairs at Sally's party." He leaned forward. There was sweat on his upper lip. "His hands were all over you. You're still intimate with the guy."

"No. We are not still intimate."

"Bullshit," he said, his voice rising. He looked down at the grass, collecting himself, and inwardly cursed her for unsettling him so fast. He looked up. Then he walked back toward the mulberry tree and jammed his fists in his pockets. "You always thought you were smarter than everyone. Better than everyone. Well, you're not and those pictures prove it."

She opened her eyes. "I don't follow your logic."

"Stop acting dumb, Page. You almost married that loser."

"You're saying I'm not smarter than everyone because I *didn't* marry him?"

"No, I'm not saying that! I'm saying you think of yourself as being better than everyone, and yet you sunk to his level for a while. It took Ellen Chevalier all of 20 minutes to get him in the sack…"

"Did you see the pictures?"

"Of course, I did…"

"They were never in 'the sack'." He stared at her; she regarded him with wonder. "She tried very hard, but…"

"Oh, shut up, Page. That's not the point!"

"The point is there are probably pictures of Ellen Chevalier all over town. They mean nothing. You missed your mark, Willis."

"Well, consider it a practice shot."

"No," she said.

"Chester was my cousin. I owe him."

It stops now," she said.

"I'm just getting started," he said smiling.

"Oh, really?" she said, smiling too. "You're not the only one with pictures, Willis."

McHugh's smile disappeared. He compressed his lips until they too disappeared. He took a deep breath, held it, and then expelled it, saying, "What are you talking about? What pictures?"

"Pictures of two houses on Beasley Road—houses that were sold for under market value to someone who had privileged knowledge that the two schools were going to merge."

He snorted noisily and waved his hand back and forth twice. "Those houses were shacks—they weren't worth the price they got."

"The land was worth a million dollars, as it turned out," said Page. "A million dollars in your bank account."

"That's how business is done, Page. It's done all the time." The mayor's tone implied she was a ninny to suggest otherwise.

"I have no doubt," said Page interrupting, still serene and erect before him. "The woman who owned the brick ranch house sold immediately, didn't she? But the old man, the one who owned the farmhouse, who had lived on the farm his whole life—he didn't want to sell, though, did he?"

"I don't recall," he said looking away.

"Sure you do, Willis. He held up the works for six months…until the merger was almost a done deal and about to become public knowledge…and then…then the old man turns up dead on a lonely stretch of road in the Gumbo Flats, his truck flipped over and he...He was found drowned in a ditch in three inches of water..."

"That was an accident!" said the mayor, turning a deep shade of red.

"Just his poor luck—but it was an awfully lucky accident for you."

"That's sick, Page, to even suggest...You don't know what you're talking about! I remember his heirs. They were torn up about it. They were more than glad to have the property taken off their hands, to unload it..."

"For $65,000."

"Something like that."

Page leaned forward, the white knuckles of her small hands the only part of her revealing the tension which surged through her body like electricity. "What a great guy you are, Willis! You were doing them a favor taking that house off their hands!"

"It wasn't that way...It's just how business is done...It's done all the time."

"If people were to hear the facts though...the whole picture..."

"The whole picture nothing! Pictures can lie, Page."

"My point exactly," she said as her amber eyes, shooting sparks, met the flat brown beans in the mayor's face. "And maybe you were right," she said slowly. "About an exchange."

McHugh took a hesitant step toward Page. He raised his arm to reach inside his jacket, but his hand hung in the air for a moment before falling open upon his chest. "You know," he said. "My old friend Ethel Weinrich once spoke to me in a similar way on the same subject. We were never able to come to an understanding, I'm afraid...before someone did her in."

"Another lucky accident for Willis McHugh?" said Page, forcing herself to smile as she felt a cold chill spread through her body and settle in her knees. She widened the set of her feet on the grass and waited.

"I guess I'm just a lucky guy," said the mayor. He reached inside his jacket, but hesitated once again.

For a moment Page nearly choked on her panic, but she held herself steady. Did he have a gun in his pocket? Would he hesitate to use it, his lifestyle threatened, his world crumbling? Could the crack of a hockey stick connecting with a ball cover up the report of his gun? Would she fall to the ground paralyzed as he smirked above her, watching the lifeblood drain from her body? Would she try to scream, her mouth forming the silent syllable, as she remembered her sons? Then her hand shot out and she wiggled her fingers. "Hand them over, Willis," she said distinctly. "Now."

"Here," he said hoarsely as he held out a folded white 5" x 7" envelope to Page. "But for all you know, these could be all over the Internet already. Any teenager knows how…"

She blinked, dismissing her panic and her daydream, and took the envelope. She pressed it against her chest. McHugh's face seemed to soften and he said, "I just meant it as a little joke." He smiled, ruining his effort to cover his feelings.

"Sure, Willis," she said. "That's how business is done. I know. You've been doing it since high school."

"Yeah, those were the good ol' days." He smiled again, remembering. Then he narrowed his eyes at her as he focused once again on their business. "But it isn't as if anyone forced that cowboy to go to her house and jump into Ellen's arms. We were just there to make it a Kodak moment. And no matter what you say about not being intimate with the loser anymore, Page, I don't believe you. You want him, and now you know you can't trust him. You'll never forget how that detective looked with Ellen Chevalier's breasts pressed into his face. Those images are burned into your brain and you'll never forget and you'll always wonder…"

"No I won't," said Page. "That's the difference between you and me. I won't wonder."

The mayor groaned and waved his hand dismissing her. "Turn a blind eye, then, and trust the asshole."

"You shall have joy, or you shall have power, said God; you shall not have both."

"Oh, that's great, Page." He turned halfway and slowly clapped his hands. "I'm so impressed the way you can quote the Bible at will."

"It was Emerson."

"Oh, sorry, fucking Emerson." He turned to the hockey field again and jammed his hands in his pockets. His shoulders came up and his neck disappeared. "By the way, Page, where did you get your information regarding my real estate dealings?"

"It's all part of the public record. It was just a matter of…"

"No. No. You had help. I know that. You're smart, but you couldn't have had time, not since this morning. Who helped you?"

"Well, I admit I was in a bit of bind time-wise," she said. "So I went to see my godfather, David Whittier."

"*David Whittier?*"

"Yes," she said. He had turned back to face her, and Page saw that her words had hit their mark. McHugh's face was scarlet, and his shoulders seemed to have attached themselves to his ears. "I wouldn't try to cross him if I were you, Willis."

"Jesus, Page, you think you're going to get away with this? Well, you've got another thing coming…"

"Do I? I guess you'll always wonder about that."

"Jesus, you're finished, *finished* in this town."

Page smiled pleasantly, thinking of Jimmy Cagney. "Goodbye, Willis," she said. "Have a nice day." Then she turned and hurried away, never pausing until she reached her car. She threw her purse and the envelope onto the passenger seat and collapsed into the driver's seat exhausted. She breathed deeply, feeling stupid for reacting so strongly. Then she remembered Elijah and her body slowly relaxed. She wiped her eyes and blew her nose. *Behold, I will bring evil upon thee, and will take away thy posterity, and will cut off from Ahab him that pisseth against the wall.* She smiled. All that wouldn't be necessary. She just didn't ever want to be threatened again.

Chapter 54

She said I reminded her of her daughter, the one who died when she was a little girl, four years old when she got sick. Her name was Ann Marie Weinrich. She said it was amazing, like a gift from God. At first she'd stare at me. She'd say, 'blue eyes just like yours, those blue eyes like china.' She showed me pictures. She looked a little like me, but I never saw what she saw. She was just so young, still with her baby fat and that wispy, fine blond hair. But Ethel saw it, and who was I to deny her what pleasure it gave her?

From the beginning she never mentioned Carl Jr. or the blackmail. She forgave me and forgot about it. She welcomed me into her home and we decorated my apartment together in blue. We put the dolls in my bedroom, the ones that had been in Ann Marie's room. They were Ethel's collection which she had started for Ann Marie and continued after her death. Beautiful dolls from all over the world. Historical dolls too, like Nell Gwyn and Mary Queen of Scots. Oh, we loved those dolls, and when we traveled, we always bought a doll or two. They were our secret, just as I was her secret, her Ann Marie. I don't think anyone knew, not even her best friends, Carol and Ruth and Peggy. Certainly Carl Jr. didn't know. He hardly remembered that he'd had a sister. He was just a toddler when she died and no consolation to his mother.

Over the years Mrs. Weinrich and I were happy together. We were simpatico. I have no family, you see, and all she had was Carl Jr. and they were never close. So we had each other. It eased her pain, her sense of having been cheated by life, I think. She could not stand to be cheated or slighted, you know. That's what the notebooks were all about. She kept score. She couldn't bear the thought of anything else being taken away from her. Not after Ann Marie and after her husband... he cheated too.

Carl Jr. was a great disappointment to Mrs. Weinrich. He was so much like his father, proving to be just as unworthy and much less discerning in business. He needed money desperately. I felt sorry for him. Truly. He was pathetic, the way he would hint around to his mother and she would ignore him. He was too afraid to ask straight out. I never thought he would try to blackmail his mother. No matter what he says, that is not why I told him about his daughter. I just thought he should know. He turned to his friend Willis McHugh. The mayor told him who to get in touch with. He handled it all on his own without help from me. His mother was outraged. We both were outraged—but she looked at me differently after that, as if she imagined I was involved.

And then...and then she started working on her will again. This time she included a lot of personal items, her own things. I just couldn't believe my eyes when I saw that the dolls—my dolls—were going to go to her granddaughter, to Julie Weinrich. My beautiful collection, all of them, all to that horrible little slut in the hammock. I couldn't believe it. I thought it had to be a mistake. So I asked her, I asked Mrs. Weinrich why, why wasn't she giving the dolls to me? Now you must understand I never had ever asked her a question about her will. It was none of my business, but she always had me check it. So I knew what was in, what was out. I asked her about the dolls. Do you want to know what she said to me? She said, 'Well, Sylvia, of course, the dolls must be kept in my family. It's not as if you are a blood relation. But don't worry now,' she said. 'You can see that you'll be taken good care of with a trust fund just for you which Carl Jr. will oversee.'

You know how they always say, something snapped? Well, something snapped inside me. All those years were nothing to her. I was nothing. I wasn't Ann Marie anymore. Her granddaughter, who never came to see her except on holidays to receive presents which I picked out, was more important in the end because she was a blood relation, because her father was a member of the Middle Essex Club.

So I thought, fine, if that's the way it's going to be, fine. I called Thurgood Pinchot. We were somewhat acquainted; Mr. Pinchot had come to me earlier. He had sensed my importance, my influence with Mrs. Weinrich. He wanted me to try to sway her in regards to the building of the new administration building. I knew I couldn't and I told him that. There was no cajoling Mrs. Weinrich when she was on a mission. No. But things had changed. Everything was different. No one would be talking about cajoling a change now.

No. I told him about the change in the will, that the school was back in. He understood immediately the need to be decisive, to take action, and he did. He never hesitated. He looked me right in the eye like I understood.

I didn't kill her, of course. Mr. Pinchot took care of everything. It all went very smoothly, according to his plan. He took care of everything. It was that George Crabtree who ruined everything by nosing around, suspicious, on Saturday afternoon. He asked a lot of questions. I could tell he knew something. He was suspicious of Mr. Pinchot. When Crabtree left, I called Mr. Pinchot. It was his idea to kill him and make it look like a suicide. He left that big party Saturday night and picked me up and we went to Crabtree's house together. He thought it was all falling together, rather than falling apart, because we could make it look like Crabtree had committed suicide out of remorse over killing Mrs. Weinrich. He said, 'Thank you, George,' when he hit him over the head. He said, 'Thank you.'

Merton leaned against the table, his arms crossed at his waist and his boots crossed at his ankles. He stared out the window, unseeing. "That's quite a story," he said finally. He turned around slowly. "But you haven't told us who killed Mrs. Weinrich. Was it you? Did you slip in unnoticed to the lunchroom? How did you get her downstairs?"

Vesba, who had been staring silently at the tabletop, suddenly came alive and slapped the wooden surface hard. Arno jumped. "Yes, how did you do that?" asked Vesba.

"I didn't," said the other woman, instinctively pressing back into her chair. "I wasn't even there by that time. All I did was drop the tarts off an hour earlier."

"Are you trying to tell me Pinchot got her to go down there?" asked Vesba leaning forward. "How could he be two places at one time?"

"Oh, he couldn't," said Arno.

"Then how?" said Merton, leaning on his fists on the table.

"It was Renzi Stark," she said matter-of-factly. "Stark killed her."

Chapter 55

There was a car outside when she arrived home, although she hardly registered the fact, she was so exhausted. But when she got out of her car, she was slightly alarmed to see the tall man outside enter the garage, his head bowed, his hands clasped and his elbows in, so he wouldn't touch her car or the bikes against the wall and get his suit dirty.

"Renzi," she said. "What are you doing here?"

He came up close to her and touched her lightly on her sleeve. "How did it go with McHugh? I was worried about you."

"It went all right I guess," she said, walking around the car and stopping at the stairs into the house. "I got what I wanted."

"Did you?" he asked. "So few of us do, if we even know what that is."

She took a few steps up, then turned and looked down at him. His face looked strange; the eyes were all wrong, like they were in the wrong face. She wished he would say, "Okay, that's all I was wondering," and leave, but she was not surprised when instead he said, "May I come in?"

She hesitated. "All right," she said and turned back to unlock the door with fumbling fingers. She pushed it open and went in.

Stark paused at the open door into the dining room. "Do you want to put down the garage door?" he asked.

"No," she said quickly. "I'm going out again soon. Why waste the energy?"

He shrugged and followed her through the dining room to the kitchen where she threw down her purse and took off her coat. She picked up a piece of paper on the island and read it. "Oh," she said. "The boys have gone to soccer practice with my neighbor." She glanced at her watch. "They'll be home any minute," she lied. She looked around the familiar room as if to regain her bearings, noting that everything was in its place. She folded the note and put it in her pocket like a talisman. "Can I get you something to drink?" she asked in as pleasant a voice as she could manage.

"No, thank you," said Stark. "Can we talk somewhere?"

She nodded and held out her hand. "The living room?" He nodded and she led the way into the front room. She sat on the couch, smoothing her skirt, her hands pausing on her knees. She did not lean back. He walked to the mantel and rested one arm on it. He drummed his fingers.

"Willis McHugh asked me who helped me," said Page. "I told him David Whittier and that seemed to stop him in his tracks. Anyway, I don't think he'll be able to connect you with any of it."

"It doesn't matter," said Stark.

"It doesn't?"

He turned to her. "It's funny, but I don't remember you from high school at all."

"Why would you?" said Page. "I was quite forgettable."

"I've tried and I've tried, but I just don't...I wish I had though, I bet you were nice. I didn't know Gussie then either. I knew lots of people, but they were all the wrong ones to know. I knew Chester." He walked around the coffee table and stopped in front of Page. He sat down on the edge of the table and their knees touched. She leaned back on the couch. He leaned forward slightly, his elbows resting on his thighs. "I asked Chester once, hey, what's going on this weekend? He said, oh, Big Doings—a huge party at Milne's house on Friday night. So I say, cool, and what do I do? I get a date with Lisa Mandrake, a cheerleader from St. Agnes. I really cashed in my chips, and you know what? When we got there, to Milne's, the house was dark, not a light anywhere. No party. Big joke. I never said a word about it on Monday. He never asked. I acted like it had never happened and it was like it never did."

"I did a lot of blocking myself," said Page. "Became quite an expert, in fact. Lots of people survive their childhoods that way. It isn't that unusual."

Stark raised an eyebrow and one side of his mouth pulled back. "Chester taught me an important lesson—that the likes of me should never ask the likes of him what's going on. Never ask. They can tell you, if they want you to know, but *never ask*." He smiled suddenly. "I let it all wash over me. Nothing ever sunk in too far back then. I was blinded, I guess, by the bright glare of my surroundings. If

I'm *here,* everything must be all right."

"What's the matter, Renzi?" Page said while concentrating very hard on regulating her breathing. She smoothed her skirt again and then crossed her arms across her chest, pulling her cardigan sweater tightly around her. "Tell me what's the matter."

He shook his head slowly from side to side. "I did everything I was supposed to. Everything. I got good grades and stayed out of trouble. I went to a good college and graduated. I even came back here and worked for my father, selling goddam Pontiacs, until he went under and sold out to Lou Otto for nothing. But I didn't let that bother me. Even when everyone else was piling up money and I was going deeper into debt, I kept going. I got married to a nice girl and made it through law school. We had kids. Things were looking up at last. We bought a house and I started moving up the Alumni Council ladder at Bingham. It seemed to me like somehow it was all connected, like it was meant to be. I'd go out there and everything was so...fine. I thought my life must be fine. People were friendly, gracious, *appreciative.* I thought they were anyway. I thought I knew them. I went to their meetings. I sat on their boards. They told me things. You don't talk to someone you don't like; you don't *share* with someone you don't trust. But I guess she was just being polite, you now. I was driving her home after all, she..."

"Who?" said Page. "Who were you driving home, Renzi?"

He blinked. "Mrs. Weinrich, of course. Several times. We had some good conversations—about her mostly, growing up in Middle Essex. But sometimes I told her about my family. She remembered when my grandfather opened the original dealership in Southtown. I enjoyed her company. I really did."

"What changed?"

"*She* changed—or she seemed to—over the trees, the park. She had to have her way. When I disagreed with her at the board meeting last month, she literally exploded. I thought she might shatter into a million pieces. But she didn't shatter. No. She looked me straight in the eye and said my opinions were 'irrelevant'. *I* was irrelevant. She said that, right in front of everyone, and no one disagreed. No one said a word. They just smiled, like finally someone had had the nerve to say what they all had been thinking all along."

She made a soft, animal noise in her throat, but he did not respond. He looked down at his hands, caught up in his own memory. "After the meeting she stopped me in the hall and started threatening me, saying she'd tell her son to fire me. She snapped her fingers in my face and said, 'just like that,' he'd do it too. She always got what she wanted, and this business with the trees wasn't going to be any different. If I knew what was good for me, I'd better step into line and fast. She was on a roll and feeling good. She looked twenty years younger."

"What did you do?"

"I went home and told Augusta. I thought she'd tell me not to worry, that Ethel could kiss my ass, but she was scared and that scared me. I talked to Buzz the next day. He told me not to take her seriously, that Ethel was just spouting. She didn't mean it. I should sit tight. But I knew he just wanted to get me off the phone. I was just a pathetic crybaby and he wouldn't lift a pinkie to help me. But I was wrong. A few weeks later he called me. He needed me. *Me.*"

"He needed you? How?"

Stark looked up at last, his eyes wide and terrified. "He needed me to kill Ethel."

Chapter 56

Vesba sat quietly at the table while Merton paced back and forth. "Rich people," she said suddenly. "Goddam rich sons of bitches."

"It's not so easy," said Merton.

"Not so *easy*?"

He stopped pacing and looked at her. "Think about it. That kid I talked to who lived behind Ethel Weinrich—he and his sister and their friends—they're as neglected as any kids in a gang, growing up on their own, fending for themselves. They're probably worse, because they have every material thing they could want—cars, money, booze, drugs. They band together because each other is all they have. They don't get any adult supervision from their jet-setting parents with their busy social lives. Their peer group—their gang—is all they have. They carry that with them into adulthood. The Middle Essex Country Club—that's their gang, and that's who Carl Jr. turned to when he needed help."

"Willis McHugh?"

"Right. Renzi Stark just wanted in. He was initiated so to speak."

"Some initiation."

Merton grumbled an agreement. "*He's* the one I don't understand. He had everything—what did he think he needed? He really *is* the loser they always thought he was." He started pacing again. "And where the hell is he now? He's not in his office. He's not home. Why can't they find him?"

Vesba shrugged. "They'll round up his sorry ass, don't worry. Why are you so tense?"

He stopped pacing. "I don't know. It's just a feeling."

"Yeah, well, maybe it didn't turn out to be who we wanted it to be, but we solved the case, didn't we? In three days no less. Not too shabby I'd say. You should be pleased."

"You don't sound so excited yourself. What are you thinking?"

"Nothing," she said. She crossed her arms over her chest and looked up at her partner. She sniffled loudly. "There is one thing."

"What?" he said uneasily.

"Well, this morning when we went downtown to see Carl, Jr., I..." She hesitated. He opened his eyes wider, urging her to continue. "Well, when we were getting off the elevator to leave, I saw someone getting on, to go up."

"Who?" he said.

"Well, I didn't think anything of it. I figured she was going up to see Whittier, but..."

"*Who*?" he repeated, as he leaned on the table in front of her and stared into her pale blue eyes.

"Page," she said quickly. "It was Page."

He flinched and stood up straight. "Why didn't you tell me?"

"I didn't want to start some big thing about Page."

"You said she'd never leave the house..."

"I didn't think she would ..."

He stepped away from the table. "Stark," he said. "Do you think she went to see Stark?"

She nodded. "But she might have been going to see Whittier..."

"Why Stark though? She said she hardly knew him. She knew his wife." He looked at her once before he grabbed his jacket off the back of a chair, which crashed to the ground. It was a look that said if anything happens to her I'm blaming you. Then he was out the door.

"Wait for me," she called after him. He didn't hear her; he didn't stop.

Chapter 57

"Why are you telling me this, Renzi?" she whispered.

"So you'll understand why I'm doing this, why I have to do this." He lowered his eyes again and slowly reached inside his jacket pocket. He pulled out a small handgun. He held it loosely in his grasp and gazed at it.

"No," gasped Page as she tried to stand up. He grabbed her hand and pulled her down again. He did not release her hand, but pressed it against her knee.

"What?" he said.

"Put that gun away. *Put it away.*"

"I'm not going to hurt you. I wouldn't hurt you. I just couldn't do this at home, you know. The kids..."

"What about *my* kids, Renzi?"

"I'm sorry."

"Yeah, I bet," said Page, wrenching her hand out from under his. "Put it away, Renzi."

"No. I have to do this. I thought you might understand."

"I don't."

"I'm sorry then," he said looking away. "No one understands. They never do."

"What about Augusta? Have you told her about...what you did?"

"No," he said quickly. "She doesn't know anything about it. She never did."

"Don't you think you should tell her?" She tried to insert a kindly note into the question, but she knew it sounded false and impatient.

"Don't you get it?" he said. His voice cracked and tears appeared in his eyes. "She's better off without me."

"Horseshit," said Page.

"What?" said Stark, squinting.

"I said, very plainly, 'horseshit'," said Page trying to stand up. He clamped a hand on her knee and held her down. "What the hell?" said Page, grabbing his hand and attempting to shove it away. "Get your hand off my knee."

He retracted his hand and she stood up. "I wouldn't hurt you," he mumbled. "I thought you would…"

"*Understand*," she said, finishing his sentence. "Well, I *don't*." She put her hands to her head and pressed her temples hard. "I doubt whether your wife will understand either how she's supposed to be better off without you, but you could have given her the courtesy of confiding in her at least and spared me. The last thing I need is you to come barging into my house to confess to murder and then blow your brains and blood all over for *my* kids to see. They've seen enough of that, thank you."

She crossed her arms across her chest and breathed deeply. Finally she allowed herself to look down at the man perched on the coffee table. He looked semi-deflated in his gray flannel work clothes, exhausted and confused. She examined her spiritual reservoir of sympathy and compassion, but found only anger rising within her. She prayed *O God, help us in the midst of our struggles…to work together with mutual forbearance and respect…*She held out her hand. "Why don't you give me the gun, Renzi?"

"Why?" he said, pulling the gun to his chest. "It's my gun."

"Okay, fine. Be that way," she said, all her forbearance draining away. "Keep the goddam gun. I just wanted to look at it."

He looked at the gun in his hand. "Here," said Renzi. "You can look at it." He reached out, handing the gun, butt-first, to her. "You can look at it."

She inspected the gun fleetingly. "It's a nice gun," she said. Then she turned and walked to the fireplace where she rested her forearms on the mantel and gazed at the gun, wondering what she should do. She glanced at her watch. *Dear Lord, he may think he wants sympathy, but anger worked in my favor. I have the gun. I need to keep him talking. How am I going to keep this guy talking? What shall I ask him, Lord?* "What was your mother like, Renzi?" she asked, her back still to him.

He snorted. "My mother?" he repeated. "My mother was an alcoholic social-climber with delusions of grandeur. At least, that's what Augusta says."

"What do you say?" said Page turning halfway around to look at his hunched back.

"I don't know. She was just my mother."

"Oh," said Page, rolling her shoulders impatiently. "Well, what was your childhood like then? Did you grow up in Rockville? That must have been nice."

"Yes, it was all right. But, you know, it's a funny thing," said Stark, half turning where he was seated and craning his neck to look at her. "I have practically no memories until I started out at Bingham. That's when my real life started."

Page stared at Renzi, straight into his blank blue eyes, her mind turning somersaults as she bit her tongue and resisted a terrible urge to laugh. The adrenaline rush of her earlier anger had sapped her energy, and she prayed for strength and courage and a spirit of self-control. Her hand tightened on the gun. The doorbell rang.

"Don't answer that," said Stark.

Page began to move immediately, bolting for the front door, clutching the handgun, ready. When he began to stand up, she turned on him. "This is *my* house. I'll answer the door!" She looked down and saw that she was shaking the gun at him. He sat down. The doorbell rang again.

She struggled with the lock and the gun, then finally pulled the front door open, revealing a Rockville police officer, his hands on his hips, smiling. "Evening, Ma'am," he said. "I was passing by and noticed your garage door is open and..." His smile faded as he noted the gun raised in Page's hand. "Is everything all right?"

Chapter 58

It was dark by the time Merton drove up to the house. The door to the garage was open and a strange car with its driver's side door ajar was parked haphazardly in front of the house. Two Rockville police cars and a County police car filled the cul de sac. He cursed and lunged out of the car.

"*Where's Page Hawthorne?*" he asked the first policeman he encountered inside the door. He scanned the living room, catching sight of Renzi Stark, hand-cuffed and about to be escorted out of the house. Before the startled officer could answer, he had grabbed Stark's collar and thrown him down. "What did you do to Page?" he shouted, falling on the other man. He banged Stark's head several times on the floor. "Where is Page?"

A hand gripped his arm and tried to swing him around as he continued to shake Stark. "She's in the bathroom," said the police officer who had followed him. "She's okay. She's had a rough day from all reports, but she's okay."

He stopped shaking the other man, but did not let go. "She's okay?" he repeated, staring at the man underneath him while he endeavored to control his breathing. He relaxed his grip somewhat, but his knee still pressed into Stark's chest.

"Yeah," said the officer pulling him off. "Everything is under control." He patted Merton on the shoulder, then leaned down and pulled up Stark, who was weeping.

"Do me a favor?" asked Merton. "Call Leona Vesba in the Major Case Squad for me. Tell her what's happening." The policeman nodded and turned back to Stark.

The bathroom door was ajar, and Merton slowly opened it. No one was there. There was a little black skirt on the floor and an ivory silk blouse in a heap next to it. Size 6 black pumps lay haphazardly in front of the toilet. Pantyhose lay crumpled on the sink. He went to the sink and moved the pantyhose. As he turned on the cold water and began to fill a glass, he looked at the jade plant on the radiator next to the sink. Dead leaves lay curled and brown on the dirt. There was a crack in the blue and white pot. He poured some water on the plant and refilled the glass. He turned around and walked to her bedroom door and knocked gently.

"Who is it?" she said.

"It's Roy. Can I come in?"

"Sure," said the voice inside.

He opened the door and poked his head in. He glanced at the bed taking up most of the space in the small room. It was covered with a blue and white quilt, which someone had made, but he couldn't recall who. She had told him once that it meant something to her, like all the things in her house. She was sitting on a window seat, looking out through the open blinds onto the street in front of the house. When he came in, she turned. She had her knees up and her arms embraced them. She was wearing very old jeans, an old flannel bathrobe and a white t-shirt.

"Are you sick?" he asked stepping over to her.

"No. I'm all right." He handed her the glass of water, and she took a sip. She smiled. "You always give me a glass of water, like that will cure everything."

"Not exactly everything." He crossed his arms, resting his weight on one leg, and looked out the window. "But when I was a little boy a glass of water meant comfort, solace. It meant someone cared in the middle of the night."

"You're a funny guy. Did anyone ever tell you that?"

"All the time," he said, sitting down on the edge of the seat. She moved her feet, giving him some room. It was a small window seat. "You've been crying," he said. "You never cry."

She put down the glass on the windowsill. She folded her arms in her lap. "When I was a little girl and I watched all those old John Ford westerns with Ben Johnson galloping through Monument Valley, I always pictured myself like that on a horse, my hair flying out behind me. That was my self-image, fearless and on horseback. But the first time I ever encountered a real horse in the flesh, I was petrified. The thing was huge, scary. There went my self-image."

"You're one of the bravest people I know."

She closed her eyes. "When we are bold, mighty forces come to our aid." She reached for the glass again and took a sip of water.

She cleared her throat. "What are you doing here anyway?"

"We couldn't find Stark. Then Leona remembered she'd seen you downtown this morning in Whittier's building, and I had a bad feeling, so I…"

"You were mean to me this morning," she interrupted. "Intentionally mean."

"I was," he said to the room.

She paused, but no explanation was forthcoming. "Well, I'm glad," she said. "That's what finally got me moving and back on that big ol' horse."

He looked sideways at her. Then he said, "Leona swore you'd never leave the house."

"What has she ever understood about me?"

One side of his mouth smiled. "Not much," he said. "So what was Stark doing over here?"

"He was looking for comfort I think," she said. "A glass of water at midnight. He wanted someone to listen and then tell him okay, I understand. He was going to kill himself."

"But why you?"

"In the middle of all this, I needed him to do me a favor. I trusted him and he was very accommodating."

"You went downtown to ask him for a favor?"

She nodded. "I needed some information about the mayor. It's a long story."

"Which you don't want to tell me."

"Not now."

"I suppose that's why Leona didn't tell me she saw you this morning. She thought I'd get side-tracked by a long story."

"Maybe so," she said as she watched the policemen leave her house with Renzi Stark in handcuffs. "Shouldn't you go with them?"

"Leona can take care of it," he said. "I didn't come here for Stark." She continued to look out the window, and he stood up and stepped over to the dresser. "Stark," he said, as if the name itself tasted bad in his mouth. "That guy had everything—a wife and kids, a home—and he just threw it away like it wasn't even important." He loosened his tie. "It's warm in here." He took a deep breath and exhaled. He rested his arms on the top and surveyed the mass of framed pictures that covered it. He picked up a small silver frame. It contained a picture of him on the beach in Jupiter when they had stayed in Sally and Phil's house at Christmas. He was asleep on a yellow and white striped towel, his head turned to one side, a blissful expression of peace on his tanned face. He turned to her, confused. "Sally says you're as good as engaged to Custer."

"Sally," she said dismissively, but not unkindly. "Billy's practically a member of the family anyway, so why not make it official? Sally would like that. I married Chester because my mother liked him. Do you think I should marry Billy?" she asked.

He laughed and placed the frame back in its spot between a picture of Tal as a baby and a picture of Page holding hands with Sally at a long-ago picnic. The sisters wore matching red, white and blue dresses and the same haircut. "No, I don't think you should marry Custer," he said looking at her. "If I were you I might be tempted to pack my bags and get the hell out of Dodge. But not to Chicago with him. You could go anywhere, Page. Take the boys anywhere. Change your name, change *their* name."

"Willis McHugh told me I was finished here as well."

He laughed again. "Did he really?" She nodded. "You must have made him very angry."

"I'm afraid so."

"I wish you'd tell me about it."

"It was no big deal," she said.

"I think it was a big deal. You did an uncommon thing today."

"What was that?"

"You asked for help."

She pried her eyes away and said, "And look where it got me: my house full of policemen."

"Including *me*," he said. "I want to think that maybe that was why it all ...happened."

"You and the indifferent universe?"

He smiled tentatively, his tired gray eyes dimly lit from within. "Maybe I'm feeling hopeful."

Chapter 59

The bed was very large and the pale pink sheets expensive. The light was indulgently dim. The two people on the bed were wearing pajamas.

"Sometimes it seems like all I do is fix shit," said the man.

"I know, darling, you're marvelous," said the long-limbed woman beside him.

He grumbled. "No one thinks I'm marvelous. I'm the guy who fixes things—not the guy who gets credit for it."

"And who would that be?"

He grumbled again. "Oh, I don't know."

"Why don't you relax, darling? You're so tense," she asked, moving her hand expertly over his chest hair. "You had some fun, didn't you? You sent those pictures to Page Hawthorne and you got the reaction you wanted, didn't you? She was shocked; she came begging."

"She came to see me, but there was no begging. I gave her the digital thing."

"You *gave* it to her?"

"Yeah, why not? My heart was never in it."

"You have a heart?" she teased.

"I must be getting old."

"Don't say that. That would mean *I'm* getting old and that's completely ridiculous."

"I just feel old. Ever since Chester died..." His voice trailed off, whether from ennui or depression, the woman could not tell.

"Maybe we should do something wild and crazy," she interrupted.

"Like what?" he said, turning to her.

"We could divorce our spouses and marry each other."

He turned away again. "I could never afford that and you know it."

"*I* could."

He grumbled. "Why bother? What would be the point?"

"We could run this town together. Think of the fun!"

"I already run this town."

"The operative word was 'together,' darling." She gave him a little slap. "We love each other, don't we?"

He laughed. "Yeah, baby, we love each other."

She hit him in the shoulder. "Made you laugh."

He pulled her closer. "I do feel better. I won't even mind going to work tomorrow. I'll think I'll fire those two detectives."

She looked up from under her lashes. "But how can you do that, dear? They'll be heroes. They did their jobs brilliantly. I already saw the fat one on the news."

He grumbled. "So what's your point?"

"You just don't like him because he's in love with Page Hawthorne."

"In love," he said with a sneer. "Maybe that's his punishment."

"Maybe that is," she said moving her hand down his abdomen. "I thought I heard that she was going to marry Billy Custer."

"That faggot?"

"He's hardly that."

"And you know this how? Personal experience?"

"Jealous?" she asked as she slid on top of him. "You do love me, darling."

C.R. Compton grew up and still lives in a book-filled house in St. Louis, Missouri. She is the author of *Holy Comfort*, the first in the Middle Essex mystery series. Married and the mother of three children, the author works at Washington University. Her hobby is time management.